I0536783

# Chasing Arlo

## Genoa Mafia Series Book V

By Ginger Ring

Chasing Arlo

Copyright © 2020 by Ginger Ring.
All rights reserved.
First Print Edition: April 2020

LIMITLESS PUBLISHING

Limitless Publishing, LLC
Kailua, HI 96734
www.limitlesspublishing.com

Formatting: Book Pages By Design
Cover Design: Deranged Doctor Design
Photographer: JW Photography
Model: Robert Kelly

ISBN-13: 978-1-64034-920-9

No part of this book may be reproduced, scanned, or distributed in any printed or electronic form without permission. Please do not participate in or encourage piracy of copyrighted materials in violation of the author's rights. Thank you for respecting the hard work of this author.

This is a work of fiction. Names, characters, places, and incidents either are the product of the author's imagination or are used fictitiously, and any resemblance to locales, events, business establishments, or actual persons—living or dead—is entirely coincidental.

# Dedication

*For my father*

# Chapter One

## *Chicago*

### *Thirteen years earlier*

Arlo

"Have I told you how much I hate parties?" Arlo Brunetti groaned.

"Yeah. At least ten times since we left the house. Relax." His best friend, Roman Caponelli, nodded and turned to face him. "We have to be here. Do you think I like it any more than you do?"

Arlo flexed his fingers. The fact they had to leave all weapons at the door just added to his discomfort. Damn, he felt naked without his knives and guns. "It's different for you."

"Really?" Roman lifted his eyebrow. "How so?"

"Come on. You're important. I'm not," Arlo spat under his breath. "Everyone is looking at you with high regard while I'm dirt. Less than dirt. These social events are bullshit, and this." He waved his hand at the crowd. "A god damned masquerade ball.

1

What the fuck, Roman?" It was actually a birthday party for Layla Rinaldi but who the hell cared. He didn't even know what she looked like. She was just another mafia princess among the many. The pampered only child of Bruno Rinaldi. All the girls looked alike with the dim light and masks hiding their eyes.

Not only couldn't they have their guns but they were required to wear masks. Talk about taking your life in your hands. This was a logistical nightmare as far as security went and that was the only reason he was there. To protect Roman. They were there to represent the Caponelli family. Roman's parents and his little sister Valentina were also in attendance but they had their own bodyguards.

The ball-slash-birthday party was the full spectrum of over indulgence. It was on the level of a mafia wedding. All the women had over done hair, elaborate masks, and beaded dresses. And the flowers. Thousands and thousands of dollars' worth of flowers and gifts. Arlo'd never seen so many bouquets and pretentious people in his life. The room reeked of roses and overpowering perfume. Even worse, as a bodyguard for Roman and soldier for Roman's father, he was expected to wear a frickin' tux. A goddamn monkey suit. At least they'd paid for the rental. Roman's, however, was custom made.

"You are important. There's no way we can ever thank you enough for what you've done for the family, but I agree. We're only here out of respect, not for enjoyment. A birthday party for some rival family's brat is the last thing I want to do today. Just buck it up for a couple more hours and then we can get the hell out of here."

"I'm bored," Arlo grumbled and glanced around the room.

"So am I, but one day, we'll be standing here at one of our kids' parties and we can laugh at how bored all the young soldiers are."

"Maybe you, but I'm never getting married and never having kids." He crossed his arms in front of his chest.

"Famous last words. You'll probably get hitched before me." Roman elbowed him.

"I doubt that. You're the ladies' man, not me."

"Doesn't mean I want to be shackled to one but I have to carry on the family name." Roman took a sip of champagne and puffed out his cheeks. "I need something stronger than this shit." He set the flute on a nearby table. They were both only twenty years old but the mob didn't have a drinking age. You were old enough to kill, you were old enough to do whatever the hell you wanted to.

"I'm bored as fuck," Arlo repeated and ripped off his mask. You'd think just getting out of prison he'd be craving the company of others but it just reminded him of the hierarchy of the joint. There he was a small fish in a polluted pond of blotted grass crap.

"I agree. I'd much rather be spending my time with a long-legged redhead. Or blonde. Or brunette. Really don't care right now." His buddy was probably picking out his next conquest right now.

"I hear ya, Romeo." It was his nickname but very

few dared call Roman that to his face. The guy went through women like a chain smoker went through cartons of cigarettes. "At least the food is good." The fact that he'd been able to sit at the table with the Caponellis was a blessing but he couldn't complain about anything they did. They were family to him.

The band started up again for their last set. Hopefully they wouldn't have to stay too much more. If he had to watch a bunch of teenage girls jump around a dance floor any longer, he'd slit his wrists.

Arlo rocked back and forth. He was on edge and needed to blow off some steam. "Fuck, how soon can we leave? I can't take much more of this."

"Look, I don't want to be here either but shut the fuck up." He raised his voice. "You're driving me crazy. Go find some girl to dance with." Roman shook his head.

"What girls?" Arlo knew he was being a dick but his patience was running on empty. If he was miserable, Roman was going to be also.

Roman nudged him in the arm. "Over there. That blonde's been eyeing you for half an hour. Now get the hell out of here."

"What about you?" Technically he was supposed to be working, not dancing. He shouldn't leave Roman's side.

"I'll be fine. I need to talk to my father anyway, so I'm going back to their table."

Arlo glanced at the area where Roman's family had gathered. There were at least three bodyguards standing nearby so they wouldn't need a fourth.

"You sure?" Maybe some female company would improve his mood. It couldn't get any worse.

"Yes, get out of here. Please," Roman added before walking away.

Arlo returned his gaze to the young women laughing and standing around the punch bowl. It was hard to tell what her face looked like but the girl Roman had mentioned kept smiling his way. He cursed under his breath and headed in their direction. Maybe spending some time with a girl his age would improve his mood but it was doubtful.

Here goes nothing. Before going to prison getting women was a no brainer. They were a dime a dozen and easy to get. Since his release, it had become more trouble than it was worth. Most wanted just a brief walk on the dark side without any further contact. For the most part that hadn't been an issue but when they treated him like he was lower than scum on their pretty shoes, that was a different story.

The closer he got, the more they giggled. "Hi." He stopped by the table.

High pitched voices responded in kind.

Arlo turned his attention to the one who seemed to be the most interested. "What's your name, beautiful?"

They squealed and he inwardly rolled his eyes. Maybe this was more trouble than it was worth also.

"Marisa." The blonde one finally spoke up. He recognized the name. She was the daughter of one of the ranking capos and way too young to be on his arm. He'd still give her a turn on the dance floor.

"Pretty name." He poured it on thick. It was a

5

pretty name and from what he could see of her face, she was also. "Care to dance?"

"I would but…" She stalled and glanced around. "…my father would never approve of me associating with someone of your rank." Out of nowhere a woman who must be her mother came to their side.

Rank. He cringed from the invisible fist to his gut. Even this young lady thought him beneath her.

"Girls, you need to get back to your table." The woman glared at him as she filled her glass with punch. "Now," she barked.

Marisa mouthed a silent apology as she was led away.

So much for being welcomed back to the family after time served. Bastards.

To save face, Arlo grabbed a cup of the fruity red punch and downed it in one gulp. He wrinkled his nose at the overly sweet drink. It was just like the women who'd just left. Too much fluff and not enough kick.

The punch and the girls were the last things he needed in his life right now but the rejection still stung? Heading for the bar, Arlo ordered a whiskey straight. The amber liquid burned going down but it felt good. It was the only company he needed right now. Ordering another one, he took the glass and exited the building.

It was a nice night and the quiet was a welcome reprieve from the music blaring inside. The moon was full, the air crisp, and there was no one around to annoy him. He stretched his back and breathed in the fresh air. Finally, he could breathe again.

He took another sip of the whiskey as he strolled along the stone balcony. The Rinaldi place was a castle, just like all the other mafia homes. A fortress to keep your enemies out and your family in. His shoulders relaxed and he rolled his head. It was a clear night and the stars were out in full force. In prison, inmates hated when the lights went out but he yearned for it. Arlo was protected by the Caponelli name so no one dared mess with him.

The evenings meant peace and not having to listen to the orders of the guards or the whining of the other convicts. Inhaling the moist Lake Michigan air again, he raised his chin and closed his eyes. Peace and fucking quiet.

A footstep on the concrete shattered the silence like a sledgehammer through glass. Arlo reached for his gun but came up empty. He wasn't alone after all.

# Chapter Two

"I'll dance with you." The female voice caused him to loosen his fist.

Arlo turned to see a girl smoking in the shadows. The red embers of her cigarette glowed in the darkness. "Who the fuck are you?" He squinted in the moonlight. "Get out here where I can see you." He was gruff but it was the first time all night he'd had a moment to himself. She'd also taken him by surprise, which was never a good thing. Had the whiskey dulled his senses or was he getting careless? If a lone girl could sneak up on him, what damage could a trained assassin do?

The girl stepped into the light and he stilled. She wore no mask and he had to remind himself to breathe. Long dark hair, ivory-colored skin, and ripe full lips just made for kissing. What a beauty! Unfortunately, she appeared too young for him but in a few years, the young lady would be a knock out. Youthful curves were accented by her tightly fitted dress and unless she had very high heels on under that skirt, the girl had long legs as well.

"Does it really matter?" Her rose-colored lips pouted.

"Yes, so either speak up or get lost."

"I can be here if I want, just as much as you can, maybe even more. So maybe you're the one that should get lost." Her pert nose rose a little in the air.

"Well, you're just going to have to deal with it because I came out to get some air." The girl wasn't a threat so he returned his focus to the opposite direction. He turned and rested his elbows on the top bar of the balcony railing. "Go find some other guy to dance with you." Arlo hoped she'd take the hint and leave.

Soon the scent of her perfume floated in the air. It was spicy and hot, like cinnamon and red hots. "Not my scene either. But I saw how they treated you so thought I'd ask anyway." She wandered near.

Arlo brushed it off but he sure didn't need a reminder from her. "Dancing is a waste of time."

Her fingers wrapped around his forearm. "I can think of a better way to pass some time."

He smirked and peeled her digits from his arm. Just the brief touch of her warm skin sent a tingle down his thighs. That wasn't good. Maybe he did need to get out more if the mere touch of a girl's hand did crazy things to his stomach. Arlo gave her a quick glance from her head to her toes. "How old are you?" She was fourteen at the most. "Does your mother know where you are?"

"I'm sixteen and my mother is dead." Her big brown eyes drew him in before she turned her gaze toward Lake Michigan.

"Sorry about your mom." Arlo straightened. He'd lost his mother at an early age as well. It sucked and was probably even a worse experience for a girl.

She shrugged her shoulders. "Life's a bitch sometimes."

"You got that right." Arlo glanced down at her before gazing off into the distance again. He was over six feet but she was only a few inches shorter. She was also long and lean, as one would expect a trained dancer or athlete to be.

"What's your name, Sugar?" Who was this girl anyway? Her lack of mother explained the lack of supervision but there was probably a father back in the room that would kill anyone who touched his little girl. At least he hoped so. The thought of her being without a protector didn't sit well in his gut.

"Sugar?" She glanced up at him and her smile melted his heart. Just a little but it softened just the same. "Does that mean you're sweet on me?"

"I like sweets but one bite of you might be the death of me." His knuckles tightened on the railing in front of him. "Cut the BS, princess. Who are you and who's your father? I don't want to deal with some jackass going batshit crazy on me because I'm alone with his daughter. I have enough problems to deal with."

The young woman rolled her eyes. "I don't need a protector and as soon as I tell you my name, you'll run to the hills. Just like everyone else." This time her lower lip trembled and he couldn't help but want to take up arms against anyone who would dare say an unkind word to her. There was

10

something about the young lady that spoke to him. Struck a chord in him. Like she wasn't judging him or his time spent in jail. Like she was on the outside looking in, just like he was. "Why don't you leave if you're so afraid of being seen with me?"

Him, afraid to be seen with her? That was a first. "I never said that. I'm not going anywhere and I'm not afraid of anything."

"That's why I followed you out." She smiled up at him and the brightness of it matched the stars up in the dark sky. "I know who you are."

"And who am I, little girl?" He tensed as he waited to hear the words, convict or ex-con.

Her eyes narrowed at his words. "Someday you won't see me as little." It was a challenge and he had to respect her bravery.

"I do now, so spill it." The cat and mouse game had gone on long enough.

"I know you're Arlo Brunetti and you just got out of prison for taking a fall for the Caponelli family." She placed a hand on his chest. "You were the brave one, not those other cowards inside."

Her comment shocked the hell out of him. No one was supposed to know he'd taken responsibility for a crime he hadn't committed. "And you're not afraid of being alone with me?"

She didn't seem to be since the young lady knew who he was. It was a nice change to not have others look down on him when he'd fallen on the sword for so many.

"No, you're a protector. A hero. You sacrificed yourself for the family. There is no truer soul than that." Turning around, she leaned her back against

11

the railing. "They should be celebrating you and offering their daughters to you on a platter."

He was shocked to hear say these things. "And why would they do that? A girl's virtue is something to be honored and kept until marriage." It may not be in the modern world, but in the mob it was. An age-old double standard that wouldn't be changed anytime soon. Men could have many mistresses and brag about it, while if a woman stepped out of line, the consequences where never pretty and frowned on heavily.

"That is so barbaric. I'll probably be sent off to some arranged marriage, intended to be some peace offering in a turf war. Do you think that is worth saving my virtue for?"

She had him there. He wouldn't wish that on anyone. Again, the husband of an arrangement such as that could take advantage of the many prostitutes in the whorehouses that some of the families maintained. The Caponellis never worked in the sex trade but he knew the Rinaldis did.

"Well, do you?" her soft voice rang louder.

"No, but that doesn't mean you should put yourself at risk. There are bad people out there. Enemies of the family, whatever the hell family you're from. They would think nothing of taking you and making you pay the price for the sins of your father."

"See?" Her eyes widened. "You're a protector. A hero out to save girls at sweet sixteen parties."

Arlo tugged at his collar. He needed to go in. Get away from this exasperating yet intriguing young woman. "I'm no hero."

12

"I'll prove it." She took off running down the stairs of the patio, her heels clicking before she stopped and tore them off her bare feet.

"Wait." He cursed and glanced at the heavens. What was she up to now?

"What for?" She stopped and turned his way. "Are you going to dance with me now?"

"Hell no." Arlo plopped a fist on the railing. Where the fuck was this girl's father? He didn't have time for this shit.

The girl spun around and started running again.

"Hey, where are you going?" He said it loud enough for her to hopefully hear but not draw attention from the ballroom.

"To the lake for a swim," she yelled.

"Lake Michigan? It's too damn cold for that and you better be a good swimmer." The lake was brutal on a good day.

"I can't swim at all." She tossed back. Her hair flowing as she ran.

What the fuck? He paced.

That was it, the girl was obviously insane and that's why her dad didn't care what she did, but for some unknown reason, he did. Arlo leaped down the stairs, took off on a run, and snared her arm before she could hit the beach. He swung her around and held her tight so she couldn't go anywhere.

"What the hell is wrong with you?" This time he took her by the arms and gave her a good shake. "Are you trying to kill yourself?"

"No, I did it to prove a point." She looked him straight in the eye.

"And what god damn point would that fucking be?" Arlo saw red. The fact that she would so recklessly sprint toward the water still had his heart racing. What if the girl had slipped and been swept away? He tried to brush it aside that he was only thinking about himself and that he'd be the one that would have to bring her lifeless body back to the party but it was more than that. The little dark-haired beauty saw him, spoke to him, and it wasn't the way that others did. She spoke his language. It made no sense whatsoever. She was a child and a crazy one at that. "Again, what point would you have to make that would be worth risking your life?"

She pulled away from his grasp and started to walk backwards to the house. "That I was right?"

"About what?" If she didn't speak up soon, he'd shake it out of her.

"That I was right. You are a protector, a hero. You just don't know it."

"I'm no such thing." He stuffed his hands in his pants pockets. Time behind bars had crippled him. Left invisible scars that she couldn't see.

"A coward would have walked away. You didn't even think, you just came to my rescue." She rubbed her arms as if cold and headed toward the house.

"Anyone would have done the same." Arlo trailed her up the steps. Determined to make sure she went inside.

Picking up her shoes, she held the railing and slipped them on. "Are you sure about that?" She stood looking up at him. There was an elegance about her, even in her youth. Arlo shrugged and glanced away. He'd been away too long if this was the way young people acted. Games were for kids and he was a man. "Arlo Brunetti," he glanced up when she called his name, "I will have that dance." She swung around and ran into the building.

He waited ten minutes before returning to the ball room. The last thing he needed was to be accused of spending time with some capo's daughter. Crazy or non-crazy. Spying Roman by the bar again, he hurried to his side.

"Where you been?" Roman lifted a beer to his lips.

"Out."

"Out where?"

"Outside getting some air." He took a seat on a nearby barstool. This night couldn't end fast enough. "Are we almost done here?"

"Yeah, the birthday girl gets to dance with whoever she wants and then we can go."

The music stopped as Bruno Rinaldi took the microphone and walked to the center of the dance floor. He made a short speech thanking everyone for coming, asking them to remove their masks, and then introducing his daughter for the final dance of the night.

Arlo did a double take when he saw who the man's daughter was. There in the middle of the room next to her dad was the same girl he'd just chased down the beach before she could jump into one of the Great Lakes. Oh, fuck. The girl was Layla Rinaldi. It was her sweet sixteen party they were at. He rubbed his eyes. How had he missed

15

that? Probably because when she'd been introduced earlier in the evening, he'd been wallowing in misery too much to notice, plus she'd been wearing a mask.

"Layla, of the many young, handsome men here tonight, who would you like to dance with?" Her proud father waved his hand at the crowd. A few guys of various ages puffed up their chests, eager for the chance. As the daughter of a powerful don, the man that caught her eye would move up the ladder fast. Young soldiers would kill for the chance to take on that role. Not to mention, she was a beautiful young woman.

Bruno bent his head to hear his daughter's response. Like all bosses he had that classic poker face that never showed emotion but even Arlo could see the man was not happy with her choice.

The man straightened and smoothed his tie. The smile that crossed his face did not reach to his eyes.

"This should be interesting." Roman jabbed him in the side with his elbow. "Poor bastard that ends up with her will have Bruno breathing down his neck for weeks to come."

"That or get promoted for taking the girl off his hands." Arlo turned away. He couldn't care less who she picked, yet he did. It'd been the first time in a long time he'd spent time with someone besides Roman who really wanted to be with him, even if it had only been for a few minutes. Maybe he was making something out of nothing, he was four years older, for Christ's sake, but in a few years… He looked back at the circus going on the in the middle of the room. A photographer stood by to catch all

16

the highlights of the evening. Circus, indeed. Arlo reached for his glass.

"I welcome you all to join in the last dance of the night but first we give the birthday girl a moment to dance with her choice. My lovely daughter, the birthday girl," he grinned in her direction and this time his love and admiration had reached his eyes, "has chosen Arlo Brunetti."

A hushed gasp sounded in the large room.

"Damn." Roman exhaled and Arlo nearly choked on this drink.

# Chapter Three

## *Present day*

### *Layla*

Layla was a Rinaldi, yet here she was again spending more and more time with the Caponellis. They were family by blood in an odd sort of way. A few years ago, there was a marriage contract set up between her family and theirs. Roman was to marry the daughter of Bruno Rinaldi. There were other business-related things involved in the union but marrying Roman was something Layla never wanted to be a part of.

Sure, he was a handsome man by anyone's standards. She'd have been respected and well taken care of for the rest of her life but that was not the best reason to marry anyone. Layla even came to Genoa to plead her case only to find out that Roman also was not interested in marriage. In fact, he'd fallen for a local woman named Madison.

Unfortunately, neither of them had any choice in the matter. It was said that if Roman didn't go through with the marriage to her, he would be killed. How barbaric! Layla craved someone who wanted to marry her, not one in love with someone else. It went so far as the wedding day being planned and the invites being sent out.

Imagine her relief, not to mention Roman's, when Madison's mother, Connie, finally revealed that Bruno was also Maddy's father. She had a half-sister! Being the daughter of a Rinaldi, Madison was able to marry the man she loved. Layla had been a bridesmaid and gotten to later dance with the man who'd never been far from her mind. A man who probably still thought of her as child, despite being only four years younger than he. She crossed her legs and slid her fork around her plate.

Today Stephanie Barclay married Dominic Scarlatti, the cleaner for the mob. That man was hot as sin and scary as hell. Layla took another sip of champagne. Her father had left her alone after the marriage between Madison and Roman but just the other day he pointed out that she was nearing thirty and should start thinking about finding a man. Madison was now a Caponelli and Layla was the lone person who would reign over the Rinaldi clan. In his mind, she needed a strong man beside her to keep things under control once he was gone. Not to mention it was unheard of for a woman to run a mafia family. She would need a fierce husband to rule beside her and protect her. Not to brag, but there was a long line of eager beavers that would love that opportunity. Yet, it was the power they wanted, not her.

Layla had learned at an early age that not all the men who asked her out were interested in her. She looked down at her bare left hand. They wanted the influence that came with their ring on her finger. Whomever she married would rule the Rinaldi empire worth millions of dollars, if not more.

Not too long ago, their biggest rival, Fedor Dubnikov, had phoned her one night to ask for a date. As if she would go out with a member of the Bratva. It was rumored mental illness ran in that family and their cruelty was legendary. How he got her number was beyond her.

The problem with Fedor was the guy wouldn't take no for an answer. He'd sent flowers to the house, which she kept. He'd sent jewelry, which she returned. When the man called for the second time, she told him she was spoken for. Layla wasn't one to ever lie but the guy was scary with a capital *S*. Even then he pressed for the man's name. She should have hung up but Layla represented her family and therefore must be civil even to their enemies. Fedor did not live by the same code. The nutjob scared her and she didn't frighten easily.

He insisted she give him the name of the man she was dating. There was no one but she had to tell him something. Layla gave him the only name she could think of that would make Fedor get off her back — Arlo Brunetti. The man she'd asked to dance at her sweet sixteen, the man she had secretly yearned for every night since, and the man currently sitting next to her at the wedding reception.

Layla risked a glance in his direction. Arlo was

nursing a brandy and tracing a fingertip around the edge of the glass. It was hard to guess what might be going through his mind. He was a man of few words. What would he do if Arlo found out he was probably a target now for being her secret love interest? It was a given she needed to alert him and Roman of that recent development before the day was through.

After her birthday party so many years ago, she hadn't seen him again until turning up in Genoa one day to plead with Roman for an out from their arranged marriage. At first, she didn't recognize him. Her girlish daydreams still pictured him as the young man who'd come to her rescue when she was at her loneliest, but he'd matured and was even more dream worthy. The guy was well past six foot and had shoulders that seemed too wide to fit through an average doorway. He'd grown a short beard. It seemed like most of Roman's crew had one now. It was as if moving to the Wisconsin tourist town had caused them all to want to blend in with the 'up north' group.

Layla looked toward the groom. Madison always joked that Dominic appeared to be a cross between a lumberjack and a serial killer. He was often seen in plaid flannel shirts and blue jeans—a stark contrast to the other guys in their designer Italian suits. Arlo tapped his fingers on the table. The man was bored. Clearly a wedding was not where he wanted to be at the present moment. Her lips parted and she leaned closer.

"Want to grab a bottle of wine and go to my room?" Layla placed an elbow on the table and a

21

hand on his thigh.

His only response was to shake his head, pick up her hand, and place it on her leg. It was a game they'd played ever since reuniting those few short years ago. He obviously still thought of her as a child and she was more determined than ever to make him see her as a woman. Sitting so close, Layla continued to study his features. To her he was handsome. He lacked the model good looks of Jasper but sizzled strength and testosterone. The piney scent of his aftershave had her yearning for a romp in the woods.

Reaching for the butter, it was hard to miss the tan forearm in front of her. His skin was tan, muscle lean, under a dusting of dark hair. Layla took a long drink of water just imagining what the rest of him would be like. Clearing her throat, she turned her attention to his face. Cold dark eyes that she'd love to see flicker with interest. A straight nose and full lips. Her eyes focused on his mouth. Whenever he flashed that sexy smirk, it nearly brought her to her knees. It was hard not to stare whenever he was near.

"What?" He'd wiped his chin with a blue cloth napkin and tossed it on his plate. "Do I have food on my face?"

"Someday you're going to fall head over heels for me." Layla continued the assault. "You know I'm right." It was her goal in life to throw the man off balance. She lusted after him like he was air. She wanted to breathe him in and forever keep him near her heart. It was hard to say what caused her obsession. Maybe it was the chase, or the fact that

Bruno would never approve of their match. Maybe it was the way he seemed to feel her, understand her. It was hard to say. Either way, he was the only man that she'd ever been truly interested in. Having been raised by her father, she was always taught to be direct but even that didn't seem to catch his attention.

"Maybe I already have." He flashed the smirk she was just thinking about before turning it into a frown.

"What?" So transfixed on him, she forgot what she'd said.

"Maybe I already have fallen for you." He winked.

"Really?" It was too much to hope that he'd suddenly changed his mind about her but she swooned just the same.

"Layla, you're a tease. I'm sure you say stuff like that to all the guys." Her hopes dashed as he shook his head and downed his drink.

"No, I don't." His comment irked her. Turning away, she pouted. This was the extent of their contact for the past couple of years. She made passes and innuendoes that he easily avoided. Sure, the man was nice, polite, even courteous as he made brief conversation but in a way it was true. Maybe she was a tease. They'd never have a chance to get to know each other better. Her home was Chicago and his was here. Two separate families that were connected yet very much apart.

"Layla, can you help us get a few things ready before we go on the cruise?" It was Maddy.

"Sure, if it's okay with my boyfriend here."

Layla nodded in Arlo's direction. Even if it would never be true, she could at least torment him a bit more and hope.

"Layla." Arlo motioned a server for another drink and shook his head. "Anyone ever tell you you're a flirt?" The twinkle in his eyes made her heart race. It was brief moments like this that had her convinced they could make something work despite the distance. There was a connection, she could feel it.

"Oh Arlo." She rose and cupped his cheek with her palm. The short beard felt soft and tempting. "I only flirt with you."

"Come on, Lay, let's go." Maddy dragged her away by the arm. When they were safely away, her half-sister whispered in her ear. "You really need to have a serious talk with him someday and tell him how you really feel."

"I do. Every time I see him, I tell him exactly how I feel." Maddy had invited her to a girls' weekend a year ago and Layla had finally told her the story of their first meeting. Her sister, always the matchmaker, had been pushing them together ever since but Arlo clearly had not taken the bait.

"Sometimes guys need to be shown instead of told." Her sister put an arm over her shoulder. "You know as well as I do that Arlo's not a talker, he's a doer."

"Well, I wish he would do me." Her face turned bright red and she quickly added, "I wish he would just ask me out on a date. Dinner, bingo, anything." Layla turned her head and was thrilled to see him still watching them.

24

"Why not ask him yourself?" Madison nodded his direction.

Everything always seemed too easy to Madison and things had a way of falling into place for her. The woman basically ran into her future husband at a coffee shop. For pretty much her whole life Layla was sheltered and not allowed to do much of anything without her father's approval. It may be the twenty-first century but the mafia had traditions that went way back. She'd followed the rules like a proper young woman. After Bruno was reunited with Madison's mother, he seemed to forget she existed, except to remind her she needed to find a husband and fast.

For years, Layla had drifted from project to project, looking for something to occupy her time and prove her worth to her father. Math had always come easily to her so he trusted her with the books and accounts. She found ways that costs could be cut and also suggested ways to make more money.

Her only true passion was dancing. Having taken lessons since she was a kid, it was the only thing she was really good at. Madison had successfully run several businesses, making Layla's contributions so far in life seem minimal.

"Hey, earth to Layla." Maddy stopped and looked her in the face.

"It's okay. I'm just a bit confused right now." Layla glanced at Arlo again, whose eyes were still focused on her.

"About what?"

"Where my life is headed." She twisted to face Madison. "I'm almost thirty and still living at home

25

yet I have nowhere to go. Father's pressuring me to marry because that's my only worth."

"Nonsense." Madison rolled her eyes.

"I have no skills," Layla argued.

"Yes, you do. You went to business school, didn't you?"

"I have a degree in accounting but what good does that do me? I have no interest in being an accountant. I did it to help with the family, just like Valentina pursued a law degree."

"You love dancing." Madison was always the optimistic one. "You could teach. Start a school."

"I took lessons for years, yes, but who's going to want the daughter of a mob boss hanging out with their kids?" Layla became more depressed by the minute.

"I would." Madison gave her a hug.

"There is one thing I'm very thankful for." Layla's gaze fell to the floor.

"Yeah, what's that?" Maddy lifted her chin.

"I'm so happy you're my sister. I don't know what I'd do without you."

"I'm happy too, and don't ever feel you can't come to me with any problem. You know I would do anything for you."

"I know." And it meant the world to her.

Madison guided her over to where Stephanie was gathering her things for the boat ride.

"And one more thing before we go." Madison stopped and put both hands on her shoulders. "I know you will figure out something you want to do and I know Arlo cares for you. He just doesn't know how to show it. Be patient and good things will come your way."

Layla nodded but wasn't so sure it was true. She'd thrown everything she had at the guy and nothing had stuck. "I hope you're right."

"I know I am, now let's get this show on the road—well, on the lake since it's a cruise." Madison waited for Layla to nod her head in agreement before kneeling to hook up the train of the bride's dress. Maddy had owned a bridal store for years so was an expert seamstress. When she was done, she rose and kissed her sister's cheek. "You're next, I can feel it." Her hand went to rest over her heart.

"That's indigestion, Maddy."

"No, it's fate and you're destined to be with Arlo."

# Chapter Four

### *Arlo*

"Another one bites the dust." Arlo pointed his glass toward his friend, Jasper, and the guy's girlfriend, Jackie. From the excitement on their faces and screams of joy, something big had just occurred. He knew Jasper was in love and wanted to make things official with the woman. From the way they were admiring the new ring on her finger, apparently, they just did. The pair hadn't known each other long at all but that didn't seem to matter to them.

It had been a day filled with love and celebration. Dominic, the family's cleaner, had married Stephanie, a former employee of Madison's and daughter of a Russian mob boss, Ivan Bravikova. They didn't usually associate with the Bratva but after Dom had won his daughter's hand the family had joined forces with the west coast family and Ivan had settled here to be with her.

Dominic really did have to win to get his bride.

Literally, the man had to fight to the death to save Stephanie from a monster that she'd been contracted to marry. It was like something out of a movie but somewhat normal for this group. The couple had been married earlier in the day but now they were enjoying a late-night cruise on Lake Genoa. Dominic and Stephanie were very private people so it was just immediate family and friends on the boat.

"It's a good day." Roman surveyed the group that was on the yacht. "I want my men to feel at home here and be vested in making things thrive in Genoa. I have no interest in ever going back to Chicago even though I must at times for business." Roman's father was still in good health but someday it would be Roman's job to run things there even though he clearly had no drive to do it. That was one of the reasons they were in Genoa, Roman wanted to get away from big city life. As far as his boss was concerned, their future was here and he'd started several booming businesses to prove it. A successful winery and restaurant just to name a few. Still Roman's father ruled over large territories in the Windy City and Roman was expected to take them over when it was time.

"How's that going to work?"

"No. Fucking. Clue." Roman returned his attention to his wife, Madison. She sat at a table with a few other ladies who were now oohing and aahing over the big rock Jasper had just given Jackie. The two love birds exchanged adoring looks and Arlo turned toward the lake. Just moments before they had enjoyed fireworks lighting up the night but now, he witnessed a flash of lightning across the dark sky. The August day had been picture perfect but there'd been talk of a late night thunderstorm.

"Sir?" The captain of the ship appeared out of nowhere and they both gave him their full attention. "I'm sorry but we're going to have to end the cruise early. The radar indicates a strong storm moving fast in our direction. I've instructed the crew to turn the boat around and head to the city dock as soon as possible."

"Our estate is close by, please stop at our dock and we'll get off there." Roman eyed Madison again, who was now pulling her wrap close around her shoulders. "Tell the guys to be ready to dock and get everything off as soon as possible." His boss headed to his wife's side and placed his suitcoat around her shoulders, dropping a quick kiss to the top of her head.

Sitting next to Madison was Layla Rinaldi. Never in his wildest dreams did he imagine that she'd be here at a Caponelli event but here she was. Again. Layla hadn't missed a one since her sister married into the family. The woman rose and walked his way. A gust of wind came out of nowhere and the turning boat hit a rogue wave head on. Several women screamed but no one was harmed.

Arlo hurried to Layla as she grabbed hold of a nearby pole. "Are you all right?" He reached for her arm to help steady her. She had the softest skin and Arlo quelled the urge to caress her arm.

"Yes. But we're turning around." Her shiny dark

hair had been up in an elaborate style but now the strong winds wreaked havoc with it and strands were coming loose. Despite sitting next to each other at the reception, the words they'd exchanged today had been few. As two of the few single people in attendance, it was as if everyone was trying to push them together or maybe it just seemed that way because it was what he secretly wished were true.

"Storm's coming. We have to dock quickly because of the lightning." He turned his head toward the shore. Roman must have called ahead as he could see a few men waiting on his huge dock to assist the guests as soon as the boat could reach it.

"What time is it?" Layla leaned near as the boat continued to rock.

Arlo glanced at his watch. Everyone seemed to rely on their phones for everything but he'd never part with the Rolex Roman had given him one year. "Quarter to eleven."

"That's a shame. I know they booked the boat until midnight but at least everyone got to see the fireworks."

"They'll continue the party at Roman's. Best to gather your things so we can all get off as soon as possible and the crew can get back to the dock." Her perfume drew him closer when he should be letting her go. Layla was never meant to be his, yet she'd taken up residence in his heart and soul ever since she'd picked him to dance with at her sweet sixteen party so many years ago.

He didn't see her again after that night until years later. To say she was stunningly beautiful

31

would be an understatement. As a young lady she was pretty, as a young woman she was the most beautiful person he'd ever seen. It turned out that Madison was her half-sister and they never knew it. The two did look very much alike. Both were tall, curvy, and had long dark hair. Whereas Madison's eyes were blue, Layla's were brown. As his boss's sister in-law, the woman he secretly yearned for was now even more unattainable.

They neared the wooden landing and the crew tossed out their lines for Roman's men to secure the large boat to his equally massive dock.

"You better get your things," he instructed again.

"All right but I have something I want to talk to you about." Layla stared him in the eye. "Later." It was one of the things that hadn't changed in all those years. She was direct and took no prisoners.

"Sure, but first we have to go. Now." He ushered her back to the table with the back of his hand firmly on her lower back. The wind was fierce and the crew was busy rolling down the plastic tarps on the sides of the boat to shelter it from any oncoming rain.

The captain opened the side door and the guests quickly exited the boat. Roman was last. He shook the hand of the captain and handed him a large envelope of cash for the man and his team. The crew waved as they cast off toward the city's main dock. Arlo and Roman stood on the landing watching the wedding guests rush toward the house. Stephanie's light dress was easy to spot in the crowd. Dominic held tight to her hand as they finally reached the patio of the house. Jasper had his arm around Jackie and Roman's sister, Valentina, walked arm and arm with her husband, Ryan, one of Genoa's finest—as in police office Ryan Donavan.

It was a mixed crew they had at the wedding, that was for sure, but they were all family. Some by blood and some by honor.

Roman seemed to be in deep thought, only his were probably for other reasons. His boss cared deeply for all his men and their families. Tensions were high right now with turf wars in Chicago between the Italian families and the Bratva headed by Fedor Dubnikov. They also had Fedor's brother, Alexander, tied up in a safe house right now. The bastard should be dead after all the sick and twisted things he'd done to a woman they found near dead outside of town and had almost done to Jackie, but Roman thought the man might be useful somewhere down the line in later dealings with Fedor. That remained to be seen.

"Let's go." His boss motioned him to go ahead but Arlo'd been his bodyguard for years and the man's safety always came before his.

"After you." Their footsteps echoed on the wooden dock and they finally reached the grassy shore. Even on Roman's land there was a shore path that went around the entire length of the lake. They'd just reached the sidewalk when Arlo noticed Layla coming back from the house. What did she need to talk to him about that couldn't wait for them to get inside?

A loud explosion sounded behind him and he tackled Roman to the ground. It was an automatic response. Heat surrounded them and the light was blinding. Layla was halfway between the house and the shore. Arlo observed her standing where she was, a look of horror on her face. His ears ached and he quickly glanced to the source of the glow to see what it was.

The lake was a ball of fire. The ship they'd just gotten off of had exploded. Not caught on fire but exploded, and was now entirely engulfed in flames. A pit formed in his gut. No one would have survived that. He drew his gun and slowly rose. Roman leaped to his feet as several other men rushed to surround them, also with guns in hand.

"What the hell happened?" Jasper was the first to speak. "Do you think that was on purpose?" If it weren't for the storm, they would have still been on that boat. All would have perished.

"Not a doubt in my mind." Roman studied his neighbors as a few came out on their lawns. "Everyone in the house and I want extra guards at all the exits," he ordered.

Dominic approached, his long hair flowing in the wind. "I personally checked that ship and it's been guarded ever since. How is this fucking possible?" His face was red and the usually calm individual appeared ready to lose his shit.

The boat had been a risky thing to do in the first place but it was something that Stephanie wanted. "Could have come in with a caterer, a bouquet of flowers, a crew member that somehow slipped on?" Jasper suggested.

"This is bullshit. We could have all died." Dom kicked a nearby plant and sent it flying into the lake. They were all in shock and needed to do something.

Ryan came running down to the shore, a phone held to his ear. "Everyone's secure in the house and I have the authorities on the way. I called the coast guard but it's hopeless that anyone could have survived." A piece of blue ribbon floated by in the water. It'd been part of the decorations. A few boards from the ship had drifted nearby but it was the site of a red and white lifesaver that nearly brought Arlo to his knees.

Layla stumbled on the grass in her high heels and Arlo rushed to her side. She held a phone to her ear and was talking to someone. Everyone and their damn phones, he wanted to break a few necks right now. The ones responsible for this disaster.

"Layla, get in the house," Arlo scolded but she ignored him and continued on to Roman. When she reached his side, she turned off the phone and put her hands on her hips. The wind was brutal and she had to be chilled to the bone in her thin dress. Arlo took off his coat and draped it on her shoulders.

"What is it?" Roman studied her. "You should be inside." Everyone with a brain could tell by her stance that the woman wasn't going anywhere.

"I just talked to my father." She pulled the jacket tighter to her body. "He was feeling unwell so cancelled reservations he'd planned at a nearby restaurant. That place just blew up."

Roman's gaze met his.

"Layla, we need to get you out of sight and into the house." Roman dragged her closer to the dock house so they had some shelter from the storm. The woman wasn't going anywhere until she said what was on her mind but at least they would be out of the wind. A rage went up Arlo's spine at the way Roman handled her but it was for her own good. As her brother-in-law, Roman did have certain responsibilities to her that he didn't.

As they neared the building, she shrugged off his hands. "I am speaking on behalf of my father."

"I will talk to him when we get to the house." They were almost shouting now to be heard over the wind and thunder.

"I am speaking for him." Layla stood her ground. "As Bruno Rinaldi's first born, I am passing on this message for him. I speak for him." She pointed at her chest. "This is the work of Fedor. This is war and we want you to win it." Layla now pointed her finger at Roman's chest. "Do you accept the challenge or do I go back to Chicago and settle this for us?"

Arlo couldn't take his eyes off the woman; he'd never been so turned on before in his life. It was hinted that Bruno had at one time been priming his daughter to take over the family but a woman boss was unheard of. With her hair completely undone, her dress whipping in the wind, and her hand clutching his jacket, she looked like a warrior. A fierce goddess.

Roman stepped closer to her. His jaw twitched as he gritted his teeth. "Challenge accepted, now get in the damn house."

Her eyes narrowed as lightning flashed again and thunder clacked as if it had just hit next door. Arlo put an arm around her waist and pulled her with him. "Come on. Let's go."

36

They all rushed to the house as quarter-size hail and huge drops of rain surrounded them. Ryan stayed by the dock house to watch the boat for any survivors that might have jumped in the water but so far there were none.

Finally inside, Arlo still did not let go of Layla. She trembled, whether it was from the cold or fear he could only guess. The guests stood around, their faces pale and eyes wide. The tension was thick and the room quiet. Everyone had been minutes away from being killed. It was a tragic end to an otherwise beautiful day.

What Fedor had started, they would finish. Arlo tightened his fists and his resolve. Not tonight, not tomorrow night, but it would be done. Someday he would stab a knife through that man's heart. The problems with the Bratva had been escalating for weeks and it had finally come to a head. Things were only going to get worse. People would die on both sides. Layla's lower lip trembled as she looked up at him. Arlo did what he'd been wanting to do forever. He hugged Layla tight to his chest and kissed her lips.

# Chapter Five

### *Layla*

Her father would be there any minute, as well as a few other high-ranking members of each family. The ones not in attendance were on high alert and guarding family interests and properties both here and in Chicago. It was anyone's guess where the Russians would strike next.

Layla fidgeted in her seat as she witnessed more and more comings and goings from the window of the library. They'd all gotten little sleep the night before.

"Layla, come sit down." Madison patted the seat on the couch next to her. "These pastries that Jackie brought from the Java Shop are amazing." She licked her fingers. "And I'm not just saying that because I'm pregnant."

Layla's heart filled with love. It finally dawned on her that she was going to be an aunt. The next generation of the family had already begun with Valentina's baby and now Roman and Madison's would be the next. "Do you know if it'll be a boy or a girl?" Layla dragged herself away from the window to grab a coffee and blueberry scone.

"No, not yet but Roman's positive it's a boy."

Settling onto the sofa, Layla patted her sister's knee and smiled. "I'm so excited for you."

"I would be too if I wasn't scared to death," Maddy admitted and took a sip of water.

"You'll be fine. Women have been having babies for years, everything will be okay." Living in a house with only her father for years, Layla didn't have the first clue about taking care of a baby either. "Valentina's a great mother and she's right next door."

"That's the only thing keeping me sane," she joked. "And when it gets closer, Mom said she'd spend more time here."

Madison's mother, Connie, had rekindled her romance with Bruno and had even moved into their Chicago home. It felt weird at first having another woman living there but their complex was so huge, they didn't run into each other that often anyway. Having a new woman in her father's life after so many years had been a good influence on him, and the man definitely seemed more relaxed and happier.

"Layla, I have a favor to ask." Her sister took another bite of her chocolate-filled pastry.

"Sure, anything you need. I'm here for you."

"Would you consider moving here for a while? To Genoa? You could stay here in the house with us."

"Ah, I'll see what I can do." She helped oversee

most of her father's businesses and there was always charity work to do but there was nothing stopping her from doing that from this location. "When Father gets done with the meeting, I'll ask if he can get by without me for a while. If so, I'll pack up some things and come back this weekend. Is Roman cool with me being here?"

"Yes, believe me, once these hormones kick into overdrive, he'll be glad to have you around to keep me under control."

Layla wrapped her arm around Madison's shoulder and gave her sister a kiss on the cheek. "You'll be fine."

"That's exactly what I told her." Jackie sat in a nearby chair nursing her cappuccino and swinging her foot. "Speaking of being fine, has anyone talked to Stephanie? I feel so bad about what happened." Her lower lip stuck out. "I think I want to elope. I can't imagine what they must be going through right now."

"It could have been worse. We all survived but yes, I feel terrible about something like this happening on their special day." Madison teared up, her emotions getting the best of her again.

"I heard Jasper mention that Roman contacted all the funeral homes in town to anonymously pay for the crew's funerals. He also is purchasing a new boat for the cruise company." Jackie shook her head. "The Bratva are the ones that should pay."

"They will." Layla stood up and walked toward the window again. "I can't take this any longer. I have to see what's going on." Her father's vehicle had just come through the gates. "Dad's here. I'm going to go see him."

"I'll wait here. Let us know what you find out." Madison placed her hand on her stomach.

"Are you feeling all right?" Now that she thought of it, Maddy's skin had felt a bit clammy.

"Yes, just a little morning sickness." She reached for the glass of water again.

"I'll get some crackers and be right back." Jackie quickly got up and left the room.

"Are you sure you're okay?" Goosebumps rose on her arms.

Madison reached for her hand. "For the first time in a long while, I'm truly scared. About the baby, about this whole mess with Fedor."

Layla crushed her in a hug. "It will be fine. Trust in Roman and trust in our father. They will take care of everything." She brushed a strand of hair away from her sister's face. "And I'll be here with you, every step of the way. I promise."

"Thanks, I don't mean to be such a baby but last night…" The woman's eyes started to tear up.

"Shh." She took a seat next to her. "Everything is fine. We're all fine." She hugged her again.

"It just made me realize how fragile life is."

"I know." Her thoughts turned to Arlo and how he'd taken her in his arms to comfort her. The kiss was brief and unexpected but his touch lingered long after he'd left the house.

"I want you to do something for me." Madison grabbed her wrist.

"Anything."

"Don't let love pass you by. Don't let Arlo pass you by."

41

"I don't even know if he likes me." That he hugged her last night gave her hope but was he just being nice?

"I know he does. Tell him how you feel," her sister insisted. "Do it or I will."

"Okay, okay." She sighed. If anything, Madison was not shy about pushing people together.

"When?" she insisted.

"What?" They were on the verge of war.

"When? I don't want you to put anything off, especially now."

"Soon," Layla promised.

"Here, I found some Saltines." Jackie rushed through the doorway carrying a box of crackers.

Madison untangled herself from the embrace. "Give me those things." She tore the box open and grabbed a handful. "These damn things better work. I can't move my head without getting nauseous."

Layla stood up and Jackie took her spot. "I'm going to see what's going on and report back. Are you going to be all right?" Madison smiled and Jackie picked up the television remote.

"We'll be fine. I'll find a chick flick for us to watch. Anything to take our minds off what happened."

Layla nodded and left the room. There was a somber mood throughout the house. Despite them all being alive and well, the threat still hovered in the air. Slowly descending the stairs, the room below her was filled with guys in suits. Some were her father's men, and some were Roman's. Even Dominic was there when he should be on his honeymoon. He had deep circles under his eyes and his long hair hung loose and messy.

Stephanie climbed the stairs toward her. She appeared equally tired. "Where's Madison?"

"In the library." Layla stopped. "What are you doing here? You just got married. Get out of town, go somewhere. We'll take care of things."

"Not until every one of those bastards are dead." Stephanie placed a hand on Layla's shoulder as she passed. She made a note to plan something special for the couple when everything calmed down. The fact that Stephanie's background was Russian must add to the mixture of emotion she was surely feeling.

Taking another step, Layla grabbed the railing when her gaze met Arlo's. He stood at the door to Roman's study. The room was grander than his office and from the large gathering of capos and underbosses, they would need that extra space.

Roman and her father were huddled in a corner talking in private. Layla hurried the rest of the way down and rushed to Arlo's side. "Any news?"

"Right now the fire department and Ryan are analyzing some of the wreckage, trying to figure out what caused the explosion. The ship had been under surveillance ever since it was booked last minute. Everything and everyone that came aboard was searched." He rubbed his face and her knees weakened at the sound of his sexy stubble. "It was obviously on a timer system. If it weren't for the storm, we'd all be dead." Goosebumps rose on her arms just thinking about it.

"I'm so sorry for those that didn't make it and their families." Remembering the cheerful

43

bartenders made her sick to her stomach.

"Don't worry, we'll make things right." He bent his head in her direction and the earthy pine scent he wore tickled her nose.

"Gentlemen, please head into the study," Roman's voice broadcast in the large room. The crowd of twenty or so narrowed as they entered the study and took one of the many chairs set up about the room.

Trailing the group were Bruno and Roman. Nearing her father's side, he turned and kissed her cheek. "I thank God that you're all right, Layla. I would die if anything ever happened to you or Madison."

A lump formed in her throat. "I feel the same way. We're all lucky to be standing here today." He nodded and turned to leave.

"I have something to tell you." She held his elbow. "Before you go in."

"What is it?" He placed his hand on top of hers.

"I don't know if this is important or not." Layla bit her lip. "Maybe I should have said something sooner but I just blew it off."

"I have a meeting now, can it wait?" He glanced back and forth between her and the study.

"It might have something to do with the bombings." Layla frowned as her father's eyes widened.

"Are you coming?" Roman called from the study door.

"Wait." Bruno held up a hand and motioned for Roman to come over.

With both powerful men standing in front of her,

44

her knees almost let out but she stiffened her spine. "I know we've had problems with the Bratva for weeks, months actually, but something happened that might have aggravated the situation."

"What are you talking about?" Roman asked.

"Fedor called and asked me out," she mumbled.

"What?" Roman was the first to speak and both men exchanged glances. "When?"

"Why did you never tell me that Fedor contacted you?" Her father said it quietly but Arlo appeared and had clearly heard as he took a step closer.

"I didn't think it was important." She looked from man to man. "He just asked me out. Months ago. It was no big deal. At least I didn't think so at the time."

"To him it was a big deal. It's an insult to his arrogant pride, and along with the disappearance of his brother, the man must have gone off the deep end." Roman exhaled and threw up his hands.

"Are you saying this is my fault?" Her hand went to her throat. Arlo remained quiet but the fingers he wrapped around her elbow told her he had her back.

"No, but it added to it. The whole family is crazy, anything could have aggravated a deranged lunatic's mind to go ballistic."

"What's he talking about?" Bruno spoke up but she couldn't face him.

"Wait, you have his brother? Alexander?" She'd heard of him but knew nothing of the man.

"We do. He brutally attacked a woman in one of their houses and left her for dead in a nearby ditch. Then he kidnapped Jackie and almost did that same thing to her." Layla's mouth dropped open. How horrible! "After we rescued her, we took him captive."

"I didn't know." She addressed Roman and went on to tell everything that'd happened, including her telling Fedor she was involved with someone else. It was the only thing she could think of to get him off her back.

"You're spoken for?" This time it was Arlo that asked the question. "By whom?"

"It doesn't matter, despite my best efforts she's still single," her father scoffed before raising an eyebrow. "Am I correct, dear?" It was hard to tell what he meant by the comment. He'd given up inviting upcoming capos to dinner at their house in the hopes of catching her eye a long time ago.

"Yes." Heat flooded her cheeks as she stared at the floor. "He called me out of the blue a couple months ago. I don't even know how he got my number. I told him no. Then he started sending gifts to the house, which I returned. When he contacted me again, I told him to stop. That I was dating someone." She threw up her arms. "What else was there to say to get him off my back?" Layla didn't need to repeat everything she'd already said but her brain was on overload. So many emotions ran through her mind. She finally risked a peek in their direction.

Arlo's usually poker face showed disbelief.

"I can't believe this. You should've told me this sooner." Bruno pointed at her.

"I know." Layla shrugged her shoulders. "I'm sorry. I had no clue any of this would happen."

"Well, now you do," her father stated. "Roman, I need a favor. I can't risk my daughter being in Chicago right now. I want her to stay here, under your protection."

"What? No." Layla shook her head. "You need me there, now more than ever."

"We already have our hands full with that Russian bastard. The last thing I need is to be worried he'll snatch you out from under our noses. If Fedor thinks you lied to him, or even worse, happens to find out the Caponellis have Alexander, he'll likely make you his main target."

She swallowed. "I thought this was a turf war?" She pressed her palms to each side of her head. It felt like it was going to explode.

"It is. They've been making small hits here and there for months, but this makes it personal. From what I hear he couldn't care less about his psycho sibling but it was rumored he wanted to link our families by marrying you," Bruno admitted. "I didn't want to worry you."

Her knees weakened and Arlo put an arm around her waist to keep her upright.

"Are you serious?" Her mouth went dry.

"Dead serious. When did he first contact you?" Her father folded his arms across his chest.

"It was early this spring, maybe April." It was hard to think clearly.

Bruno cursed and turned to Roman. "The end of April was when the garage was hit."

"No, no, no." It was too horrible to even think about. Her turning him down nearly cost the life of everyone she loved. "Please don't say I caused this."

"You didn't." Roman spoke up. "It's just another thing we have that he wants." She frowned at being called a thing. "Sorry, but it's true."

"I will kill him with my bare hands," Arlo declared beside her. "Tear him apart piece by piece until there is nothing left."

"I was hoping you would say that." Bruno focused on Arlo. "If you have him in sight, shoot to kill. Roman said you're the best." He shook his head. "I never thought I would say this but I want you to be my daughter's bodyguard." He glanced from one to the other. "And Layla, if he contacts you again, you tell someone immediately. Is that understood?"

"Yes," they both said.

"I will talk with you more later but for now we have a meeting to attend." Bruno headed for the room but Roman remained where he was.

"I need you inside," he addressed Arlo. "Layla, can you go stay with Madison until we're done?" It was on the tip of her tongue to argue, she'd been intent on being in on the meeting. Even though she was a woman, she was still the Rinaldi heir, but right now the stress of it all was too much. Layla nodded that she would do as told and Roman left.

"I'll be right in, boss," Arlo told him as Roman entered the room and shut the door behind him.

"You should go." She was numb and still in shock.

"I should do a lot of things but right now my main focus is you." He took both her hands in his.

Layla stilled and glanced up at him. "I'm fine.

You need to do what's best for the family."

"I need to do a lot of things but we almost lost you last night."

"We all could have died last night." She shook her head and paced the room. "And in some way, it might have been my fault."

"You know this is the life. Shake it off and don't worry. You did nothing wrong."

If only that were true. "Maybe if I'd done something sooner, said something sooner, this could have been prevented."

"Layla, it's not your fault." Arlo stepped in front of her. His nearness calmed her, his strength always a comfort. "Understand?"

The phone in her pocket buzzed and she jumped. Pulling the cell out, she glanced at the screen and muffled a scream with her hand.

"What is it?" Arlo put his hands on her shoulders and Layla handed him the phone.

***Fedor: You should have said yes. Next time you won't be so lucky.***

# Chapter Six

### *Arlo*

Wrapping his arm around her slender waist, he pulled her close. The look of fear on her pretty face was too much to take. She was always the one who teased and taunted him relentlessly. But did she mean any of it? Feel anything for him? Right now, he didn't care. Layla was scared and she was one of the bravest women he'd ever met.

He'd seen the message from Fedor. It was cruel. He was a monster and placing the blame on an innocent woman was a coward's way. The man was weak and twisted. If the bastard wanted to go after someone, go after him. Making a target out of a woman in the family was a cheap shot. Layla's hand tightened on his lapel. He needed to distract her, bring her out of her self-defeating plunge into darkness. She wasn't to blame, no one but the Bratva was.

Ever since last night, Arlo couldn't take his eyes off of her. He could have lost this precious woman without ever having her. Sure, he'd have been dead also, and probably in hell by now, but the thought of never getting the chance to taste her lips again didn't sit well. It had been an impulse reaction and meant to take her off guard.

Her beautiful wide eyes gazed up at him. Arlo paused for a moment in case Layla would say no but that response never surfaced. He placed his lips on hers. Kissing her was paradise. Her lips were full and her mouth tasted of sugar and berries. Her body pressed against his was a dream he never thought would come true. They were never meant to be together and she, in his mind, was destined to be with someone better and more important than him.

Right now, he didn't give a damn. In this moment in time she was his and he was kissing her. It wasn't a passionate, tongue down your throat kind of kiss. It was more of an I'm staking my claim, you're mine now, kind of kiss. I'm your protector, and I will die for you, kind of kiss.

His hold tightened and her breasts pressed up against his chest. Having this woman in his arms felt like heaven and earth just became one. They may be miles away in status and rank but in his mind, she would be his even if it was for just this one moment.

Someone cleared their throat behind them and he reluctantly broke away. It was Jasper. He closed the door behind him and approached the pair.

"Everyone's waiting and Roman won't start without you." The smirk on his face said he'd seen it all and would enjoy tormenting Arlo the rest of the day about it. He smirked and wandered closer.

51

"I'm supposed to stay with Layla." Arlo reluctantly loosened his hold but still had his hands on her forearms.

"I was here when Bruno said it." The guy could be an arrogant jerk when he wanted to. "I'm pretty sure he said bodyguard, not lifeguard. No need to give her mouth to mouth." Jasper laughed and ran his fingers through his perfect hair. The prick.

"I know what he meant but I can't leave her out here on her own." Truth was, he didn't want to leave her at all. She was more than safe in the house but that's what they'd all thought about the ship. How did security miss that?

"They're waiting. Bring her with." He opened the door and motioned them in.

"Women aren't allowed." Arlo didn't like it but it was the rule. He'd met some very strong women that could be just as ruthless as men.

"They are today. Bruno changed his mind and said to bring Layla with you." Jasper again signaled for them to get moving.

He and Layla exchanged glances and she finally shrugged her shoulders and followed Jasper's lead. Not the way he wanted to end their first, well second, kiss but they would be discussing it later.

"What's this?" Arlo heard someone ask as they entered the study.

"Since when do we have women in here?" It was one of Bruno's capos, Antonio or Alonzo, something like that. The guy was a dickhead to speak up and show disrespect.

"Since I asked her to." Bruno pounded his fist on the desk. "Anyone else have a problem with my daughter being here?" The man made eye contact with everyone in the room and they all shook their heads or looked toward the floor. "Good. We're trying to figure out the cause of the Bratva's grief with us and she may have something to do with it." Her father went on to state Fedor's pursuit of Layla and the timeline of it. This caused even more rumbles.

The meeting lasted a mere thirty minutes but it seemed more like an hour. It'd hardly seemed worth it for everyone to travel there. Roman's father had remained in Chicago and was on speakerphone. Everyone was tired and on edge but it was important to look everyone in the eyes and see where they stood on things.

Nothing much had been resolved except for everyone to keep their eyes and ears open. Changes would be made to shipment timings and locations. They were to vary their activities and practices. The Rinaldis were the most vulnerable, being in Chicago and closer to their enemies. The clubs would have extra security. The girls who worked there would be on high alert and there would be extra precautions to make sure they arrived to work and home safely. It may have been Alexander who attacked the woman found outside Genoa but they wouldn't put it past Fedor to take his rejection from Layla out on someone else.

She'd said little during the meeting except to respond to a question about what had caused her to attract the attention of the Bratva leader. Layla just shook her head and responded that she'd never met the man in her life. It was clearly a way to gain territory without fighting for it. Fedor was a coward. A weakling. Those who were afraid to get their hands dirty, often struck at those they thought least likely to fight back…thus, the extra protection for the women at Bruno's strip clubs and brothels.

"So, this is it?" It was Antonio who spoke up again. "We came all this way for this? Give the Russians the girl and everything will be fixed." All eyes turned toward Bruno as the man's face went bright red. Arlo swore he saw a puff of steam come out of the man's ears. Why Antonio was being a bitch to his boss right now was anyone's guess.

Bruno stood and you could hear the soft click of the grandfather clock in the room ticking as he approached the man. "Let me get this straight. You want me to give my daughter to a madman?"

"It's clearly what he wants. As one of your men, I would have been killed at the restaurant if you hadn't cancelled." Antonio pulled at his collar. "It would be in the best interest of the family to not make matters worse."

"Worse for whom? My daughter?" Bruno flexed his hands and a vein seemed to pop on his forehead. "As one of my men, it's your job to die for me and my family, and yet you want me to just hand over my dear girl to a madman?" He grabbed the man by the ears. "Well, do you?"

"Sorry, I spoke out of turn." The man lowered his gaze to the floor. "I had little sleep last night."

Bruno slapped the man across his face. The noise vibrated around the room. If Arlo had to guess, they might be wiping blood off the wood floor before this was done. "Maybe I should give them you to play with?"

Antonio continued to stare at the carpet and sweat started to bead on his upper lip. "I apologize again. I spoke out of turn."

"Get out." Bruno gestured toward the door. "I will deal with you in the car."

The man stood up and rushed out of the room.

"The rest of you can leave also. I need a moment with Roman." Attendees rose and shook hands with both Bruno and Roman. It was a show of respect and solidarity.

As soon as the room cleared, Jasper and Arlo headed to the door. "Wait," Bruno called. "Arlo, a word." Jasper nodded and closed the door behind him.

"What's up with your man?" Roman addressed the elephant in the room. Antonio.

"I think he's using." Bruno rubbed his chin. "I'd kill him this moment if he wasn't my nephew." He shook his head. "Imagine suggesting giving up Layla. They practically grew up together."

"You need to handle this today," Roman insisted. "He's a loose end. Either deal with it or I will."

"I'll drop him off at a rehab on the way home. Antonio won't have a choice. Get his head on straight or we'll cut it off. Literally."

"Anything else?" Roman rubbed his eyes. They were all tired and needed a good night's sleep.

"Yes, like I said." This time the mob boss addressed Arlo. "Layla stays here. You are to look out for her." He shoved a finger in Arlo's chest. "Touch her and it will be something else that I cut off on you."

"Bruno, your daughter's an adult. She can be with whoever she wants," Roman argued.

"You got one point in that sentence right." He turned back to Roman. "She's my daughter, and if the child you're expecting is a girl, you'll feel the same way." Bruno winked and for the first time that day, smiled. "Boys are so much easier than girls."

He hugged Roman and before he left, Bruno stopped and placed a hand on Arlo's shoulder. "Keep her safe, that's all I ask."

"With my life," he promised.

Arlo leaned his shoulder against the study doorway as he witnessed Layla argue about staying in Genoa. "I need to go home first. Make sure the businesses are all okay. I don't even have my clothes."

"If you need anything special, Connie will send it to you, otherwise buy it here."

"For how long? And what will I do here?" His heart numbed that she was so adamant about not staying.

"For as long as you need to be." Bruno hugged her and then did the same with Madison, who was now standing next to both. "Maddy, dear, your sister will be remaining in Genoa indefinitely."

"Wonderful." Madison bounced on her toes and sported the biggest smile on her face that he'd seen all day.

"But Father, the businesses. Who will oversee the girls and the books?" Layla trailed her dad toward the door. Now that the meeting was done, the man seemed eager to leave.

"The girls will be fine and you can monitor the books from here."

"I'm used to working. What will I do all day?"

The whole thing reminded him of the last scene from *Gone with the Wind* where Scarlett asked Rhett, 'where shall I go, what shall I do?' Only Bruno did give a damn about his daughters.

He stopped in the entryway and placed his hands on her shoulders. "Layla, you can do whatever you want. Start a business here if you're bored. I've got to go." He kissed her forehead. "I love you, now be a good girl and do as I say."

She nodded and watched her father get in the car and drive out the gate. Maddy wandered over, shut the door, and guided her sister back to where the guys waited. "I know this isn't Chicago but I hope you will love it here."

A weak smile crossed Layla's lips. "I'm used to working. What will I do with all my time?"

"We'll figure that out another day. Come let me get a room ready for you."

"No." It was now his turn to get into the conversation.

"What do you mean, no?" Madison tried to hide a yawn as her husband came to her side.

"Layla stays with me." Arlo took a stand. "You said you told Fedor you were seeing someone."

"Yes," she fidgeted with the ring on her index finger, "like I said it was the only thing I could think of to get him off my back."

"I doubt he would let that stop him." Arlo folded his arms in front of his chest.

"I picked someone no one would mess with."

Her eyes darted around the room. Everyone stood waiting to hear her answer.

"And who was that?" he asked.

"Like I said, the only person I could think of that would cause him to give up."

"Layla, who?" Arlo exhaled and shook his head. Madison and Roman watched the exchange beside them.

"I told him I was dating you."

# Chapter Seven

### *Layla*

He was even quieter than usual. There'd been a small shit storm after she announced Arlo as the boyfriend she'd told Fedor. Could anyone blame her for picking the one man she wished for? Not to mention the guy had a reputation as large as Paul Bunyan's blue ox. They called him 'The Shredder' after he used a cheese grater on some poor guy's arm to get him to spill his guts. A person would have to think twice before messing with the man and she probably should have also.

No, she would never fear him. She knew her secret crush had a soft spot for her also. Arlo'd even kissed her today but what was that really about? It was the last thing she had expected him to do. Clearly, he was trying to keep her mind off everything that had happened. He'd done that and more but did he mean anything by it? Did he care about her romantically? Layla slumped in the SUV's plush leather seats.

After her confession, there were a variety of reactions from the people still gathered at Roman's home. Jasper laughed out loud and slapped Arlo on the back. After that he yelled, "I knew it!"

Jackie then came into the room, and after a hard stare from Roman, the two left in a hurry. Arlo just ignored the guy and focused his attention on her. Was he displeased? As usual it was hard to tell. Roman appeared tense but that was normal for him. Her sister, on the other hand, couldn't have been happier. She bounced up and down so much, her husband grew concerned. Maddy was probably designing a gown and planning their wedding...only this time there would definitely be no cruise.

Roman basically threw them out the door saying he didn't have time for the drama and Maddy needed to rest. The overbearing brute. Since when was she a drama queen? Layla pouted. The mob boss said if she told the Russians they were a couple, then they'd better start acting like one. Being Arlo's woman was something she yearned for but being forced to be wasn't what she'd had in mind. Arlo'd not given them a choice, thus, her reason for being in the vehicle on the way to Arlo's home, and he didn't look happy.

Layla risked a glance at the man behind the wheel. Arlo was unreadable. If he were a book, the pages would be blank. For the last few years, she'd pursued him to no avail. Whether he responded to her because he had a fondness for her from years ago or something else, she had no clue.

"Are you going to say something?"

"It is what it is," he mumbled and turned into the parking lot of a huge condo along the lake.

Letting out a huge sigh, she rolled her eyes. "Is this where you live?" It was nice, very nice actually if the outside was any indication. From the looks of the other vehicles in the lot, it was expensive as well.

"For now." His lack of conversation wore on her nerves.

"What's that supposed to mean?"

"I just moved here. Used to live downtown, but after Jasper moved in here with Jackie, he told me there was a vacancy so I took it." He put the vehicle in park and turned off the key. "Don't move." Arlo got out, looked around, and then came over to open her door. "Get out."

She hesitated.

"Now," he insisted.

"Don't move. Get out," she mimicked but did as told. "You sure are bossy."

"Just doing my job." He closed the door behind her with a slam. "I'm supposed to protect you. Nothing more, nothing less." He ushered her in the building and up the stairs to the third level.

"Don't they have an elevator?" Layla worked out every day but the lack of sleep last night had left her exhausted. Not to mention her feet were killing her. The strappy high heels looked great in the store but beauty came with a price.

"Of course, but those things are a death trap waiting to happen."

Again, she rolled her eyes. The man took his job seriously but this was ridiculous. "I doubt that

61

Fedor has a hitman hiding in your building."

"I didn't think so either but that was before you told me we'd been dating for months." They reached the door of what must be his apartment. He motioned for her to stand to the side of the door and he did the same while unlocking it. After taking another look down the hall, he drew his gun and shoved the door wide open. Dragging her by the hand, Arlo pulled her inside and slammed the door. She shadowed him while he checked the place. When it was all clear, Layla tossed her purse on a table and collapsed on the couch.

Her eyelids weighed a ton. Closing her eyes, she nearly fell asleep. A nudge to her shoulder brought her wide awake. "Here, drink this." Arlo towered over her with a tumbler in his hand.

"What is it?" She took the glass and sniffed it. It was filled to the brim.

"Whiskey. Now." The leather chair creaked as he settled in the seat across from her.

"What's with the attitude?" Layla winkled her nose and took a small sip. A shiver rippled through her body.

Arlo brushed a hand over his hair and she took the moment to study the man across from her. Exhaustion was written all over his face. His shoulders were slumped in the chair and there were bags under his eyes. Even tired, he still caused her heart to soar. His full lips always made her stomach flutter and just thinking about that kiss…

"I'm fucking tired. While you ladies went to bed, we stayed up all night." He took a deep breath and placed first one and then the other foot on the table between them. "We made sure the authorities had recovered all the bodies and we went over all the surveillance tapes from the dock."

"Did you notice anything?" Unbuckling the ankle straps of her heels, she slipped her aching feet out of the shoes, and placed them on the table next to his.

"No, nothing." Resting an elbow on the arm of the chair, he leaned his chin on a fist. "It doesn't make sense."

"How so?" Taking another sip, the liquid burned going down her throat but her limbs started to relax.

"If they wanted us dead, we'd be dead. It's too much of a coincidence, something doesn't fit."

"Do you think they know about Alexander?" It was the only thing she could come up with except for the fact that if she were dead, he couldn't gain their territories by marrying her. Then again, with all of them dead, it'd be easy to go in and just take it.

"Good possibility but no one outside the family knows about that."

Choosing her next words carefully, Layla drew her toe closer to his foot. "What if it was someone inside the family that leaked his whereabouts and ours?"

"Roman keeps a close eye on who and what does everything." Arlo rubbed his chin, the scruff of his whiskers nearly causing her eyes to roll back in her head. The short beard just added to the sexiness of the man. "But…"

"But what?" Layla set her glass on the table. The condensation caused it to move on its own.

"Just a feeling that you might be right." He reached for her glass and finished off what was left.

"I know Maddy said he has cameras all over town. Does he have them here?" She'd grown up being watched but they didn't have them in her home. It made her adjust her skirt just thinking about being watched.

"They monitor all the exits and hallways but there's nothing in our apartments," he volunteered before yawning. "So, you don't have to worry about us appearing to be a couple."

"Who says I'm worried?" This time she trailed her toe up his pants leg. Did she have no shame? Guess not.

Arlo shook his head and picked up his phone, obviously trying to ignore her advances.

"What are the plans for the rest of the day?" Not an anxious person, Layla still wasn't used to just sitting around.

"We are to stay here and you are to make a list of everything you need from home and send it to Connie." His eyes reflected the light from his screen but he never looked up as he spoke.

"Aren't you going to show me around?" She arched an eyebrow but he still ignored her.

"What's there to see?" He finally raised his head and let out a deep breath. "We're in the living room, the kitchen is the room with the stove in it."

"Smart ass." It wasn't like him to act this way. "I meant if I am staying here, where do I sleep? What am I supposed to do?"

"You can take the bedroom."

That got her attention. "I thought you'd never

ask." She winked.

"I didn't. I'll sleep out here and you can bunk in there."

Layla plopped her head back on the couch.

"And as far as what you're going to do, Bruno is sending your laptop. He wants you to keep up with your businesses here." It was like she was just a chore to him and it was pissing her off. For weeks, months, years, she'd pined for the man and he was treating her like a job. A freakin' job.

"Can I ask you a question?" Layla put her feet on the floor and leaned her elbows on her knees.

"Yeah." He finally set the cell phone to the side.

"What's with this?" Waving a hand between the two of them, Arlo shrugged his shoulders.

"What do you mean?"

"Ugh. Arlo, you know I want you and yet you never take the bait." He turned his head to gaze out the window. "And then you kissed me today, out of the blue. What's up with that? Do you like me or what?" There, she threw it out on the table along with her heart and her pride.

"I was trying to distract you." He shifted in his seat. "Take your mind off things."

"That's all?" Her heart just dissolved like bath bombs in a tub of water.

Arlo groaned, got up, and wandered over to the window he was suddenly so interested in. Layla rose and followed to see what was so exciting with the view. It was a nice spot to watch the lake but nothing different than at Roman's.

"No, it's not. I'd almost lost you without ever having you. I had to taste your sweet lips just once

65

before I die."

That brought the smile back to her mouth. He did care. Layla leaned her head on his shoulder.

"But right now, your safety is my main concern. My only concern, and I can't be distracted by anything else. So, until we figure out what's going on, this relationship stays the same as it always has been and should be."

Layla stood back. "What do you mean, as it should be?"

"Look, Lay, you're the most beautiful woman I know. Any man would be the luckiest man in the world to have you but it isn't me." The pained expression on his face took her off guard and she took a step back.

"You don't want me?" she whispered.

"Of course, I do. What man wouldn't? But you're out of my league." He turned and strode to the kitchen. 'The room with the stove' echoed in her mind. Following, she witnessed him grab a take-out menu from the counter and slide it her way. "Hungry?"

"What the hell does that mean? Out of my league?" She'd gone from hurt to pissed again in 2.5 seconds.

"You're the daughter of a don. Mob princesses don't marry beneath them." He placed both hands on the surface in front of him.

"So, you thought about marrying me?" she questioned while pretending to read the menu.

"I would never disrespect you by thinking of anything else." At least he was being honest. "You are the kind of woman a man builds a life with. Not

66

the kind to sleep with and toss away."

"I don't think you're beneath me. No one does." Her lip trembled just thinking that he thought that way.

"Your father does and nothing will change that. I won't disrespect you. I won't have things halfway. In this family, when you find the woman you want, that's it. All or nothing."

She pondered his words. This was the most personal discussion they'd ever had together and she took a moment to let everything sink in. He did care.

"Until this is over, I have to keep protecting you as my main focus. Please don't try to distract me and get both of us killed. Agreed?"

When she didn't answer he reached across and lifted her chin with his finger to stare into her eyes. "Agreed?"

"We'll see." It was a challenge and one she would win. If Arlo thought he could keep things from getting serious between the two of them, he had another thing coming.

# Chapter Eight

### *Arlo*

He was beyond tired and if he thought he'd get any sleep with Layla staying in his home, that wasn't happening. She was in his town, his home, his bed, and always in his mind. Just thinking about the woman he craved being so near, and yet so far, caused his heart to ache and his head to throb. Well, it wasn't just his head that was throbbing. He'd had a hard on ever since she'd walked through the door.

Having nothing to sleep in, Arlo told her to pick whatever she wished from the closet. Was the woman curled up in one of his cotton t-shirts or had she chosen a long sleeve dress shirt? It was hard to tell, the woman always surprised him and he was dying to know. Maybe she slept in the nude. The thought of that nearly caused his eyes to roll back in his head.

Just like the meal they'd just shared together. Not trusting to get food from anywhere, he'd picked Firenza. The Caponelli-owned restaurant had excellent food and there was no fear about it poisoning them. Arlo totally expected Layla to order a sushi, soufflé, or some lightweight shit like that. She blew that theory out the door and went all out.

He'd taken a much-needed shower while he left the selection to her. Imagine his surprise when Jasper and Jackie had shown up with their food and joined them. Not only had Layla ordered enough food for an army, she'd invited them to dinner as well.

They'd dined on wedge salad, steaks, baked potatoes, and cake. It was good company, and as the evening went on the tension of the previous night had faded. Jasper had teased that since Arlo and Layla were going to be spending so much time together, he was going to start calling them Laylo, by putting their names together. They all had a good laugh about that and as much as he hated to admit it, Arlo really enjoyed it. He could get used to nights like that and that was something he'd never thought he would say.

Layla was a good influence on him. Always being a loner had hardened him. Friendships were few. There was ice in his blood but when his thoughts turned to Layla, she flowed under his skin and melted it all away. Sure, he'd spent time with the guys over beers and burgers but never had he dreamed of a dinner with another couple at his place. That was what normal people did. Not Arlo Brunetti.

He enjoyed their company and it was on the tip of his tongue to invite them again but Arlo held off.

It was all too much, too soon. Near tragedies can change a person, but things like this had never affected him before so why should they now?

Arlo yawned and sat up. Sleep should be easy to come by but he was still on edge. Adrenalin was a hard bitch to calm and she'd been surging through him like lightning ever since the boat blew up. Another hit was coming, it was just a matter of time.

"Ah, fuck." He rose and padded on bare feet to the fridge and opened the door. That damn cannoli cake dared him to take another bite. It was the best thing he'd tasted in a long time. Arlo pulled out the plate, set it on the counter, and took a fork from the drawer.

The utensil was halfway to his mouth when the door of his bedroom opened and Layla poked her head out.

"Are you eating cake?" She was drowning in one of his green and gold Packer shirts. The sight caused him to drool more than any dessert, even the cannoli cake.

"Great choice on the team." He pointed his fork her direction before shoving a heaping piece of sugary goodness into his mouth.

"What can I say? The Bears suck." Layla approached and put her hands on her hips. The gesture exaggerated her tiny waist in the large garment. "Are you eating that directly from the pan?" Her eyes narrowed.

"My place, my cake, my rules. Got a problem with that, sweetheart?" He put the cake back on the counter.

"Yeah, I do." She narrowed her eyes and was at his side in three steps. "Didn't your parents ever teach to share? Give me a fork."

Arlo did as he was told and she dug in. Putting a large forkful in her mouth, she moaned with pleasure. The woman of his dreams this close and wearing next to nothing was going to be the death of him.

"You should be sleeping." His fingers gripped the counter as he tried to concentrate on the food and not the woman.

"So should you." Layla faced the living room where his makeshift bed lay. A pillow and blanket was tossed on the leather couch. "How do you even fit on that thing? Seriously, you take the bed and I can sleep on the davenport."

Her giving his couch a fancy name just reinforced how different they were. She was royalty and he was a peasant. "No. You're a guest." He slid the plate her way, tossed his dirty fork in the sink, and wandered back to the other room.

Hoping she'd get the hint; Arlo sank into the 'davenport' and pulled the blanket across his chest. The refrigerator door opened and closed but the door to her bedroom never did. His worst and best nightmare just collided as Layla took a seat on the coffee table in front of him.

"I can't sleep and I'm cold," she whispered. "Can I sleep here with you?"

"There are extra blankets in the closet or I can turn the air down." He tried to sound distant but it was useless. She had already bewitched his heart and soul.

71

"Please." Her plea broke him. "I know I come across as brave but for the first time in my life, I'm scared." Reaching her hand out, she quickly withdrew it. It broke him, she broke him. "Truly scared."

He pulled her toward him. Lying down, he positioned her in front of him on the couch and covered them both with the blanket. He didn't need the warmth, his flesh burned wherever they touched. Layla said she was cold so he'd burn in hell to keep her warm.

"Try and get some sleep." Arlo wrapped his arm around her waist and pulled her tight. The couch was big but it was still a tight fit for the both of them. It probably would've been best to use the bed but that would have been too much temptation. He wasn't a saint, never had been, never would be, but tonight she needed him and he'd give whatever it took to make her feel better.

"Thank you." She squeezed his hand and entwined their fingers.

Taking a deep breath, he inhaled her sweet scent. She smelled of cinnamon and honey. Layla had always been sugar, spice, and everything nice, and the years had just enhanced that. He closed his eyes and the last thing he expected to happen, did. For the first time in a while, he'd slept.

The smell of coffee woke him with a start. Someone was in his kitchen. Arlo reached under the couch and pulled out his gun. Sounds of a woman humming brought everything back. It was Layla. Putting the Glock back in place, he threw the blanket off and headed toward the sizzle of bacon.

"Good morning, grumpy." Layla held out a mug of joe, little waves of steam rolling off the dark liquid. She'd pulled her hair back in a messy bun and wore no makeup. It was a different Layla than he was used to seeing and if he had to pick, he liked this one best. On her feet were a pair of his socks. They were huge but obviously kept her feet toasty and warm.

"Why are you calling me grumpy?" Pulling out a stool, he settled in the chair to watch her cook. There was no limit to the talents this woman processed.

She waved a spatula and shrugged. "Well, you aren't a bubbly kind of guy, but the look on your face when you came in the room was even more than the usual expression of gloom and doom."

He grumbled and scratched his chin. The scraggly beard needed to be trimmed.

"What's the problem?" Layla flipped a piece of bacon onto a paper towel-covered plate. "I'm assuming it's me."

"In a way." Arlo took a sip from his mug. Was it just her or was this the best cup of coffee he'd ever had? Just the right amount of sugar and creamer. And something else. "What's in this?"

"Cinnamon. You don't like it?" Her mouth dropped open.

"No, no. It's great. I like it." The corners of her lips turned up.

"But you don't like having me here."

"I never sleep the whole night. I'm a light sleeper and yet you got up, made breakfast, and I never woke. What if someone would have broken

73

in?" Damn, he'd messed up.

"You were worn out and we're in a secure location. You needed it, so don't complain." Piling some pancakes on a plate along with the drained bacon, she slid the dish in front of him. Gathering some juice, maple syrup, butter, and milk for their meal, Layla made up a plate for herself and took a seat next to him. A man could get used to this.

"Still that doesn't excuse it." The pancakes were light, fluffy, and so delicious. "Thanks for the breakfast, this is really good. I didn't know you could cook."

"I can do a lot of things good." She winked and the little minx was back.

"Still, I'm calling your father and telling him you need someone else to guard you."

Layla dropped her fork and it clanked on the service top. "You trust someone else to follow me around?"

Arlo puffed out his cheeks and rested his elbows on the counter. "No, I don't."

"Then I don't want to hear any more about it. You hadn't slept for shit and were exhausted. If we were anywhere else but here, I don't doubt that you'd still be up." She took a drink of juice. "I've already sent out an email to Connie to pack everything I need and it'll be here in a few hours."

It looked like she would be staying and he had to admit, he was secretly relieved. He really didn't trust anyone else with her. To keep their hands off her and to protect her. If anyone was going to struggle with both, it would be him.

"I will continue to monitor our businesses and

accounts from here but I need to find something to do outside of this building or I'll go nuts."

"I'll talk to Roman. He owns several businesses around town. It shouldn't be too hard to find you something to do. Madison has a lot of charities she works with."

"Thanks, but I found something." The glimmer in her eye told him she'd already decided and there wasn't a damn thing he could do about it.

"Yeah, can't wait to hear what that is." He humored her and tried the bacon. Again, it was cooked to perfection just like the rest of the meal.

"Well," she rested an elbow on the counter top, "you know how I love to dance."

Yes, he knew that. He remembered Madison once commented that Layla had taken dance lessons of every kind for years. The dance he'd shared with her at her sweet sixteen was one of his most cherished memories. They'd floated across the floor like they were professionals. He knew only basic steps so it was all Layla. She made him a better man.

"Yeah, you want to open a school or something?"

"Something." There was that gleam again. "I was looking online and saw a business outside of town that was for sale."

He racked his brain trying to think what that could be. The family and the MC had a few businesses outside town that he was familiar with but none that Layla would be interested in.

"And that would be?" Arlo poured himself a glass of milk.

"The Genoa Gentlemen's Club."

The carton nearly slipped from his hand. "That's a strip club."

"I know." Layla's face lit up like a kid at Christmas time.

# Chapter Nine

It was no use saying anymore, Layla clearly had her mind made up. Arlo glanced her way as they drove through the entrance to Roman's estate. A strip club was no place for a lady but she'd already discussed the purchase with her father. She even had a meeting set up with a realtor today to view the place.

He'd been there once with Jasper to do a collection. The owner's drug problem tended to burn up his profits instead of paying bills, it was no surprise when the place went under. The Gentlemen's Club was the last place he wanted to go today but where Layla went, he went.

First, there was a meeting with the guys to go over the latest news on Fedor. His companion would be spending time with her sister while the men planned their next move. This situation had everyone on high alert so the sooner it was over, the better. Then he could send Layla back to Chicago and end the misery of being so close to the one he wanted but couldn't have.

Parking by Jasper's vehicle, Arlo came around to assist Layla. They could be under surveillance by Fedor anywhere so they intended to keep up the game. He reached for her hand and shut the door behind them. Her skin was so soft and smooth it felt like silk. When she wrapped her arm around his waist, he felt about ten feet tall. Arlo had never begrudged the other guys finding love and pairing off but now he did. To have such a special woman by his side was just too much to wish for. However, not just any woman would do. Only Layla would.

It was instinct alone that caused him to kiss the top of her head as they strolled to the house. Even though it wasn't real, for the moment he would pretend it was. Play the part of happily ever after.

"I could get used to this," Layla purred. She'd always pursued him but whether it was pity or just a twisted yearning for someone not of her league he had no clue. Maybe it was a rebellion against her father's wishes. Her father hated the sight of him. Roman had been Bruno's first choice for his daughter but since then, there'd been no suitors that he'd heard of. Why was that?

Dominic drove in behind them. The slam of his van door broke his train of thought and Arlo waved in greeting. "Dom."

"AR," Dominic called back. They had a lot to discuss today but how much they could say and who would hear it had everyone off their game. Layla's suggestion that it was an inside job had stuck with him.

Jasper opened the front door. The guy was always an eager beaver and had probably arrived a half hour before. "Come on in, slackers." No one could blame him for wanting to do a good job.

"Jasper, you're such a brown nose." Dominic punched him in the shoulder. Despite their differences in the way they did things, they'd become close friends over the past year.

As soon as they entered the house, Madison rushed up to hug Layla and drag her upstairs. At least having Lay here was a comfort for Maddy.

"Come into the study." Roman stood in the doorway of the room. As soon as they entered and took their seats, he shut the door. It was just the four of them. Roman, Jasper, Dominic, and himself. "I've had the room swept and the cameras turned off." Certain rooms in the house had always been monitored for security but now they were concerned about the breach coming from within. Nothing and no one could be trusted.

"Did they find anything?" Dominic asked. "Who did you use?"

"There was one bug and I had Ryan do it."

Arlo sat up a little straighter. "Ryan?"

"Yeah, he had equipment from the department and if there's anyone that I trust outside the men in this room, it's him."

They all nodded. Ryan could be trusted and had saved their asses many times already. "Any leads on where it came from or how it got here?" Jasper crossed an ankle over his knee and folded his arms in front of his chest.

"It was one of ours." Roman tossed a pen on the desk and leaned back in his chair.

"So, it is an inside job?" Just as Arlo'd thought.

"Who and why? It didn't make sense. Do you think it is really Fedor and his pursuit of Layla? Or something else?"

"The Russian's an asshole." Dominic entered the conversation. "Even if he no longer wants her, he'll keep it up until he's dead or has her in his possession. Too stubborn for their own damn good." Dom's wife had been contracted to marry a member of the Bratva but escaped, only to show up years later after catching sight of his former fiancée on a social media news site.

"Then he'll be dead soon because that isn't happening." Arlo was prepared to fight to the death, just as Dominic had to keep that woman safe.

"Do you think he knows about Alexander?" Jasper suggested.

Roman entwined his fingers and lay his fist on the desk. "That's exactly what I think. I think the reason he tried to go after Layla was not to marry her but to use her as leverage to get him back. We've talked about this before. Since the Rinaldis didn't have a clue that we had him, he went after them to get to us. Thankfully, Layla didn't fall for the trap and Bruno didn't encourage it either. Even a simple date for coffee could have dragged her into something that would have been hard to get out of without a trade for his psycho brother." Arlo wrapped his fingers around the arms of his chair. his knuckles went white just thinking about her in the hands of that fucking bastard.

"And the bombings?" Dominic was obviously trying to figure out all the angles just as much as everyone else. The guy wasn't usually at meetings, as he preferred to just wait until things were over and then clean up whatever was left behind. But this was a serious threat to everyone involved. The fact that they hit on his wedding day probably didn't help either. "How does that tie into things? If he wanted us dead, we'd be dead. All there'd be left to do is just drive in and take it all. Doesn't make sense."

"If we were dead, he still wouldn't know where his brother was." From the looks of the dark circles under Roman's eyes, he'd not slept much.

"So, how many people know where he's being held?" Arlo'd stopped at the safe house a week ago. They had a three-man crew that took turns watching the prisoner and making sure that he stayed alive. Alex had attempted suicide a few times when they'd first captured him but seemed to have settled down since then. The family's doctor also checked on Alexander once a week and monitored his meds. Prescription drugs had kept the man calm and helped battle some of the guy's mental issues, making him much easier to handle. If only Alexander's brother would have done the same. Paranoia, depression, and numerous anxiety issues were just a few of the medical problems the man had.

"Just Doc, those at the house, and everyone here in the room," Roman verified.

"What about the tech guys? They monitor everyone's location through their phones." Jasper brought up a good point. It was an advantage to know where everyone was at all times but anyone with that information could use it to do great harm.

"I had Ryan set up a scrambler there. Whenever anyone gets within a half mile of the place, their signal stops at any of the various stores, restaurants, or gas stations in the area." Their boss had thought of everything, but then Roman always did. Still, the timing of the bombs going off was just too close for comfort.

"Again, what about the tech guys?" Arlo didn't want to let it go.

"I have them working overtime changing things out and gathering data. In the meantime, I want you to check them out." Roman slid a file in Arlo's direction. "It's everything I have on everyone who works in IT security. Don't overlook small details. If they lived anywhere that makes you suspicious, been anywhere suspicious, dated anyone suspicious. I want no stone unturned."

"Got it." Along with the file, his boss gave him a large envelope to put everything in. Any eyes that might be on them as they left would never know what was inside.

"Anything else we can do?" Jasper leaned forward as if ready to jump into action.

"Keep your women close and don't go anywhere isolated alone. Any loved ones that could be taken and used against us is a target, warn them as well. Also vary your routines. Do what you usually do on Monday, on Wednesday, and so on."

"What about the businesses?" Again, Jasper spoke up. His new fiancée worked at the Caponellis' winery.

"Ryan has hired some private security to help out there and at other locations." Roman looked each guy in the eyes. "Anything else?" When no one spoke up, he continued. "Be safe and be on alert. That is all."

Except for the scraping of chair legs on the floor, everyone was silent as they got up and left the room. Dominic exited the house without another word. Jasper followed behind. Roman went in the direction of the kitchen, leaving Arlo on his own.

The file in his hand was light but the weight of its responsibility was not. Their IT department was a well-oiled machine that they relied heavily on. If it wasn't for Christopher alerting them that Jackie was missing, they'd have never found her, or captured Alexander. It tied his stomach up in knots just thinking about it, yet he couldn't wait to go through the report and see what he could find.

He glanced at the clock on the wall. Damn, they had to get to the club soon to meet with the realtor. That was the last thing he expected to be doing when he agreed to keep Layla safe. It just reaffirmed the fact that you could take the mob princess out of the city but you couldn't keep the mob life out of the girl.

Women's voices could be heard in the distance. They were probably talking about names for babies or some such. Climbing the stairs, he walked the short distance to the room the sounds were coming from. When he heard his name, he stopped. They were talking about him.

"You spent the night in his arms?" Maddy sounded excited.

"Yes and no. We were on the couch but I never felt so safe. I just wish…" Layla trailed off.

83

"I know he likes you, it's just his pride in the way. You were once engaged to Roman."

"Don't remind me. Ugh," Layla blurted. "Not that there's anything wrong with him. You guys are the ultimate power couple but I don't want to rule the world."

"Rule the world?" Madison laughed and Arlo could just imagine her shaking her head and rolling her eyes.

"You know what I mean."

"No, I don't."

"I'll explain it then, dear sister. Arlo is a mystery to me. He's tough, strong, smart, and I haven't the slightest clue how to get him to see me as just me. Not Bruno's daughter, not mob royalty, none of the crap that he seems to have a hang up with. I want him to see me as a woman. To give me a chance."

"He does see you. I know he does. I see him watching you," Madison agreed. "There's no mystery about how he feels about you. I can see it the minute you walk in the room. He only has eyes for you."

"But I want more than for him to be watching from a distance."

Arlo should have made his presence known but hearing that she might have feelings for him left him frozen on the spot. She wanted him. Him! Arlo leaned against the wall, closed his eyes, and gave thanks to whatever strange twist of fate had blessed him with a such an amazing woman.

"I want to have mad, crazy, amazing sex with the man," she squealed. "And then I'll go back to Chicago and marry whoever my father wants me to."

What? His pulse stopped. He was sure of it. He couldn't move, couldn't breathe. Arlo'd been shot, stabbed, and tortured a time or two but nothing had ever hurt as much as what he'd just heard. Urging his legs to move he took a step back and then another. As quiet as possible, he retreated to the railing and down the stairs. If he had a heart, she'd just reached into his chest and pulled it out. Gripping the rail, the room swam as he made his way to the study.

For being a strong man, he felt sick. Sinking down in a chair, he leaned his head back. He'd keep her safe but after that, Arlo was done. No more mooning over someone that only wanted to use him. He was done. If this was what heartbreak felt like, love could go fuck itself.

# Chapter Ten

## *Layla*

"Did you just say what I thought you just said?" Madison's mouth dropped open.

"That I want to have mad, crazy, amazing sex with the man I haven't stopped thinking about since I first laid eyes on him. Yes." Layla put her hands on her hips and tapped her toe on the carpet.

"No, not that part. The bit about marrying someone our father picked."

"Oh hell, no. Of course not. I just said that to see if you were paying attention." Layla paced back and forth. "That ship sailed a long time ago. Father will never pick out a husband for me again and he has no say in who I choose either."

Maddy wiped the back of her hand across her forehead and sat down. "Wow, that's a relief."

"Sorry, I shouldn't be taunting you when you're in the family way." Excitement surged through her. "I can't believe I'm going to be an auntie! Either you move to Chicago or I'm moving here because I want to see the baby every day."

"Well, my home is here, so you marry Arlo and buy the house on the other side of us."

Her sister placed her palm on her stomach. Whether she realized it or not, the gesture was sweet. It had always been just her father and her so the growing family was something she'd never thought was possible.

"I'm trying but he's being all honorable and shit."

"Yes, it's horrible that he's so honorable and wants to put your safety first."

"You know what I mean."

"It's just weird seeing you pursue him when I'm used to seeing it the other way." Maddy laughed.

"What can I say, I love a challenge."

"As long as you want him for the right reason and not because he's proving to be hard to get."

"Oh, that reminds me. I have to be somewhere." She hugged her sister. "I'll call you later."

"I'll be here."

Layla started to the door.

"Hey, Lay?"

She stopped and leaned against the frame. "Yeah?"

"Go get your man." Madison grinned.

"Planning on it. Love you." And she did. It was hard to picture living anywhere but Chicago but this place and the people here had grown on her too much to resist.

An hour later, Layla wondered if her quest of being with the man of her dreams was just that, a dream. He'd hardly said two words since she found him sulking in the living room. Maybe sulking wasn't the right words. Arlo seemed distracted. Angry. Brooding.

"Are you sure everything is all right? Did something happen in the meeting?"

He drove into the lot of the Genoa Gentlemen's Club and parked next to the only other car in the lot. "Nothing to worry about."

Arlo turned off the car and this time she didn't wait for him to come around and open her door. That resulted in a scowl but it was the most emotion he'd shown since they'd left the place. If he was going to be difficult then so would she.

A big Lincoln with realtor signs on the doors gave no doubt that their agent was there. The long-legged blonde leaned against it and smiled. As soon as they got she stepped away from it, her hand outstretched.

"Hi. I'm Vicki Samuels." She kept her hand out until both of them shook it. The woman had perfectly styled blonde hair and wore a navy jacket and red skirt. "Let's go inside." Vicki had obviously unlocked the place before they got there and quickly held the door open wide. "I'm so excited to show you this wonderful business opportunity."

Vicki was there to make a sale but the last thing Layla wanted was a high-pressure sale pitch.

"I bet." Arlo spoke under his breath. "This place has been listed for what? Three months now." He spoke up loud enough for both to hear. It was obvious he didn't want her to purchase the place, maybe that was why he was in a bad mood.

"Yes, the previous owner had some personal

issues and was forced to sell." Vicki led them through the bar area. "But as you can see, the equipment is all fairly new." Except for all the alcohol being gone, everything else looked to be in place. Glasses, bar tools, even the drawers held clean, crisp towels neatly folded. Walking over to a wall, their guide flipped the light switch, bringing the stage area to life. The poles were shiny and the dance floor spotless.

"Oh, this is nice, but all the furniture will need to be replaced." Layla weaved her way between the tables and chairs to inspect the stage floor, music equipment, and lighting system. She even stepped on the runway and gave the stripper pole a good shake. It was sturdy as hell.

"It also has a full kitchen, although they never served food here." Vicki studied the notes on her phone. "All stainless-steel appliances and subzero refrigeration."

"Why'd they never use them?" That seemed odd.

"It was originally going to be a supper club but they ran out of money before it could be opened, then the second owners bought it from the bank and made it into a gentlemen's club."

"I want to see that and everything else that goes with it." It was perfect but if Layla blurted that out, she'd never get a fair price. Yes, the club would need some work but it was actually better than she thought it would be. Some of the features, such as the nude pictures in the men's bathroom, were a little on the cheesy side but she envisioned something more than just a strip club. No, her vision ran more to a high-end club with burlesque shows and ladies' night. Maybe even a prohibition theme. She practically buzzed thinking about the endless possibilities.

Arlo paid more attention to structural details, which was nice. What did she know about water heater capacity, electrical issues, and structure damage? From the frown on his face and lack of complaints, it appeared everything was in good working order. As soon as they were finished, she was getting to the bottom of what was up his ass. 'Normal Arlo' was the strong, silent type. 'Bad mood Arlo' was a bear on steroids.

They continued their tour with the office being her least favorite. It would need to be gutted. Cigarette and pot smoke still lingered in the air. That wouldn't do at all and it would need to reflect her more feminine style. The dressing rooms were okay but not classy at all. Mirrors would need to be refurbished as well as locker and make up areas updated. As they continued the showing, Layla calculated what it would cost for updates and what she was willing to pay.

"So, what do you think?" Vicki flashed a bright smile as she swung around in a flamboyant turn. "It's a great deal, so I wouldn't wait."

"I'm interested but only at the right price." Layla studied her figures again and stated her proposal. Vicki had her game face on and didn't bat an eye at the below price offer.

"That's way less than what the owner is asking." Vicki frowned, folded her arms, and twiddled a pen between her fingers. "I'm sure he could be persuaded with more money."

"Anyone can be persuaded with more money," Arlo added his two cents. "I know what he paid for this place. He'll be breaking even with a little left over. Call him. Believe me, he'll take the bid."

Layla turned his direction and lifted an eyebrow. She'd all but given up on getting any support from him.

"Call him," Arlo repeated.

Vicki took a deep breath. "Fine. I'll be right back." The realtor marched out of the building to make her phone call in private.

"What's wrong?" Layla wasn't leaving here without an answer.

"Nothing." He blew her off.

"There is, so spill." Stepped into his space and placed a hand on his chest. "Now."

"Why are you doing this?"

Even with her high heels on she had to tilt her head up to see him. "We already talked about this and I know what you're thinking, that it'll be competition to Firenza, but I promise, it won't be."

"That has nothing to do with it." He turned his back on her, walked over to the stage area, and took a seat.

How dare he walk away from her? Her heels echoed in the empty room. The chair screeched as she yanked it back and plopped herself down on the seat. "Then tell me. Now." She could play tough guy just as much as he could. "And we're not leaving here until you do."

"Why are you buying something here if you don't plan on staying? Are you going to run it from Chicago? You'll have a business in Caponelli

91

territory."

"I never thought about it being in Roman's terrain but we're family now. Once the baby's born, I plan on being here all the time." Bruno and her were going to have to talk. As his only heir they did need to clear a few things up. He planned on her taking over the business but would the men want to follow her? Would the man she married support her in being the boss? Would he be willing to support her in the decisions she made?

"What about your husband?" Arlo rested an elbow on the table.

"What husband?" Layla knew what he meant but she needed more time to get him to finally fall in love with her.

"I don't have one." She wiggled her eyebrows in a come-hither expression. "Yet. Want to apply for the position?"

Arlo rolled his eyes and leaned back in his chair. For one that was usually so cold and emotionless, his face was a kaleidoscope of emotions. A variety of shock, anger, and hurt. Something was wrong, very wrong.

"What?" Layla had had enough. "Spit it out." She placed her palms up on the table but he remained silent. "Look, I don't let my father order me around as far as my personal life goes but I do seek counsel for business affairs." Digging her phone from her purse, she sent a quick note to Roman asking permission to start a business on his ground and one to her father explaining what she wanted to do. "There, messages sent to my father and Roman. Everything is covered now. Happy?"

"That's not what I meant and not what I heard." The softness of his voice struck her as odd.

"Heard?" What was he talking about?

"I came up to get you and overheard you talking to Madison."

Wracking her brain, she tried to recall what he may have heard to cause such a riff. "Can you give me a hint?"

"You said you'd marry whoever your father picked out for you and that means you will be going back to Chicago. So, there is really no reason to put down roots here."

"That's what you heard me say?" Layla felt a thickening in her throat. "What else did you hear?"

He looked away and mumbled. "Just that?"

"Nothing else?" Oh, God. They were talking smack. It wasn't meant to be heard by anyone but the two of them. "Just that?" Biting her lip did nothing to relieve her anxiety.

"Was there something else I wasn't supposed to hear?" He directed his attention back to her.

"Of course not." She blew him off and climbed the three steps to the stage. "We were just talking about the baby. Maddy's so nervous, I told her women have been giving birth for years. Nothing to worry about." Rambling on as she walked, Layla grabbed hold of one of the stripper poles.

"You still haven't answered my question." Arlo was now looking up at her from the floor below.

"What?" She bit her lip. Did he hear the part about him?

"If you marry, he's not going to want you living here in Genoa." Arlo's dark eyes appeared nearly

93

black and his cheeks were rosier than usual.

"Jealous, are you?" Layla took a stroll around the pole. "Maybe you should marry me."

"I heard you say you would marry who your father wants you to and he fucking hates me."

"Does that mean you're interested in that position?" She slid her back down the pole. Oh, how she wished that was true.

"No." His denial echoed in the room loud and clear. Despite all her attempts, he still thought of her as a child. "I'd be a fool to fall for someone who's a tease and destined to be with someone else. Just like you said."

Layla rose and narrowed her eyes. "You obviously didn't hear the whole story. I was joking. I will marry who I want, when I want, and no one will tell me otherwise. I made that perfectly clear when Roman married my sister. My father got his merger and I am free to choose who I want. If you would have stayed any longer, you'd have heard that despite being an asshole who escapes my advances every time he can, it is you I want to get to know better and no one else. Happy now?" It pissed her off to have been caught saying stuff she shouldn't have.

Arlo shook his head and marched over to the bar where he pulled his phone out and studied the screen.

A buzz from her cell stopped her from chasing after him. Both Roman and her father had given their okay to purchase the place. Slipping her purse over her shoulder, she prepared to leave as Vicki came back into the building. "Great news. It's a deal if you still want to make the offer."

Layla held out her hand. "It's a deal."

# Chapter Eleven

### *Arlo*

His stomach growled as they took the elevator up to his apartment. It had been a long afternoon. While Layla did her thing, he had a chance to study the files and one thing stood out. Despite the large salary they paid, one of the tech guys had an empty bank account and lots of debt. That was never a good sign. He'd sent Roman a message with his concerns.

After that they'd gone from the club to the bank to the realtor's office. It was a done deal. Layla now owned a strip club outside Genoa and there wasn't a damn thing he could do about it. What Layla wanted, Layla got. Except for him.

Before he really didn't care if she'd bought it but now it would be a constant reminder of her when and if she went back to Chicago. Actually, it wasn't a when and if, it was just a when. He'd heard what he heard and there was no way she could skirt around it. The woman was a tease. How many other men did she have strung along? It was hard to think of her that way when she'd only ever been kind to him but some people had a dark side. He surely did. The right thing would be to just let this go but he'd had a hard-on for the dark-haired beauty for years. Even if it was wrong, he wanted her even if it was just once, even if it was for all the wrong reasons.

Risking a peek in her direction, Layla seemed just as distracted as he was, only her mind seemed to be zeroed in on her new acquisition. The day should have bored him to death but any time spent with Layla was never that. As soon as they stopped Layla was out the door. They were safe in this building but he needed to caution her on letting him exit vehicles first.

A plan had formed in his mind during the long afternoon. Layla had spent years chasing him anytime they were together. Basically, throwing herself at him, but he wouldn't be made a fool of. He'd always considered himself a gentleman as far as women went. They were to be respected and treated with kindness but this was different. In all these years, he'd tried to be the honorable one but no more.

If she wanted a plaything, he would be just that. He would be the one that made her fall in love with him. Arlo could be charming when he wanted to be and the rest, he would make up along the way. Jasper and Dom could advise him on everything else. If Dominic could bring a girl with him on a cleanup job and she still married him, it couldn't be that hard to do.

Maybe it was the taste of forbidden fruit that got

Layla all hot and bothered. Maybe she liked slumming with those who were beneath her, like a Romeo and Juliet type of shit. Their families were united, especially now that both were targets of the Russians.

Layla used the access key he'd given her to enter his place. He followed and shut the door behind him. She was ignoring him and it pissed him off even more. Whether it was done on purpose or not he didn't care right now.

"Hungry?" Arlo tossed his keys and they slid across the counter.

"Hmm?" Her nose was still stuck in her phone, the light from the screen reflecting on her face. It was the first time he'd seen her appear vulnerable but it was just an act.

"I said, are you hungry?" Leaning his back against the counter, he studied her from across the room.

Her head remained in place as her eyes looked up at him. "Yes, what did you have in mind?"

"Do you want to go to the Pier?" When she tilted her head to the side, he elaborated. "It's a nice place to eat."

Turning off her phone and stuffing it in her purse, Layla stretched her arm along the back of the chair she was sitting in and crossed one long leg over the other. The image of her draping those long limbs around his waist briefly flashed through his mind. "Is this a date?"

There it was again, the tease. The femme fatale. This time he was ready for her. "Do you want it to be?"

The expression on her face was priceless. Her eyes widened and her mouth dropped open. Slowly she nodded, as if afraid she'd misunderstood what he said. "I do."

"Then get dressed," he suggested. "Do you mind if I use the shower first?"

Again the hesitation, as if she didn't know whether to shake her head or nod. "Ah, you go first. I just have a few things to finish up first." Pulling her computer to her lap, she stole a look his way before starting to type away.

Chuckling to himself, Arlo went into his bedroom but the sight of some of her things on his bed stopped him short. He'd never brought a woman here so as luck would have it, the woman he wanted most was the first to ever sleep in his bed. Unfortunately, she slept there alone. A touch of guilt popped into his brain before he could quickly send it on its merry way.

Before this was over, he would sleep with her. He would have her in any way that was possible. If he had to go to his deathbed regretting the mere fact that he'd made love to her just once it would be worth it. She was a drug to him. An addiction he'd been able to control. Until now. A secret yearning that should never be. If Layla knew why her father hated him, she'd join him in that loathing. By then it would be too late. He'd have had his fill and be happy to send her on her way.

He took a deep breath and let it out. His fingertips touched the lace nighty that lay on his pillow. Her things had arrived and were draped everywhere. Who was he kidding? Happiness

99

would never come his way. He'd been dealt the losing hand as soon as he was born. Not able to resist, he brought the silky fabric to his nose. It smelled of her. Sweet, spicy, and oh so sexy. Regretfully, Arlo let it slip through his fingers and back onto the bed. Happily ever afters were for others, he'd have to settle for love by deceit and hope it didn't kill him in the long run.

The shower helped, the warm water flowing over his body and down his legs. It should have been cold because all it did was make him think about her. Layla touching his body and making him hard in all the right places. He reached for the knob and turned down the hot but the chill just made him want to seek the temperate dark-haired woman in the other room more. Giving up, he braced a hand on the wall and reached for his dick. A few strokes and he was spent, breathing hard. He finished the shower and grasped a towel.

Arlo dressed quickly in grey dress pants, a crisp white shirt, and light jacket. It was still warm out but he couldn't risk people seeing guns holstered under his arms. Combing his hair back, he took one more look in the mirror. Not bad, if he did say so himself. Maybe when he was done with Layla, he could find a nice girl to settle down with. Who was he kidding? After he was finished with her, there'd be nothing left of him. As much as it hurt to admit it, she was all he wanted. This whole charade was an excuse to pretend to have something he never would.

Layla squealed when he opened the bathroom door and walked into the bedroom. He'd caught her getting ready. A dress was halfway over her head and gorgeous body.

"A little help here," she yelled.

"What happened?" On closer look he could see she had the back zipper tangled in her hair. "Hold still and I'll try and get you unstuck." Carefully he pulled the strands from the metal teeth and pulled the dress lower. It finally settled on her shoulders and he zipped her up.

It was a pretty orange dress with flowers here and there. Very unexpected from the fierce business woman he was used to. Her attire tended to be bold colors of black, red, and blue.

"What do you think?" Layla surveyed the look in the full-length mirror. "I would have never tried this on in a million years. The saleswoman picked it out and I decided to give it go."

"It's nice and you look beautiful." He'd said it without thinking. She was beautiful. A garbage bag would look hot on her.

Her puzzled gaze met his in the reflection. He'd thrown her off balance. But then a smile appeared on her face. "I think you're trying to get me into bed, Arlo." Her delicate hand cupped his jaw as she revolved around.

"Isn't that what you've been hoping for years?" Wrapping his arms around her waist and pulling her close, it felt right and natural but their relationship was anything but.

"Yes, but you've always been the mature one. Why now?" She leaned into him and laid her head on his chest. "What game are you playing?"

"I know we're supposed to pretend to be a

couple but what if we really were? I don't mean just sex. I want the whole thing. Your father be damned." Stepping back, he guided her chin up with the tip of his index finger.

"I'd like that. Tell me more."

"If you are to be mine, I'd want all of you and nothing less will do."

Her eyes sparkled. "Are you serious?"

"Yes, of course." A tinge of guilt spiked in his gut. What if he was wrong and she'd really did care? Did he want to take the risk of hurting her? The memories of what she said echoed in his ears. How could he forget that it was her who just wanted to use him before going back to Chicago and the bed of whomever they decided would be the best match for her. What a crock of shit.

"But you always turn me down." Layla narrowed her eyes and brought him back to the present.

"Maybe you wore me down." He flashed her a smile but it didn't seem to work. "Life is short. Maybe it was the thought of losing you without ever having you that changed my mind."

"You have no idea how long I've waited to hear you say that." Layla put her arms around his neck in a hug.

A pierce of guilt edged down his spine. She sounded too hopeful to be lying. What if he was wrong?

"I can't believe we're actually going on a date." Layla smiled so big it lit up the whole room.

"Then let's go. I'll call ahead so they have a table waiting." Untangling himself from her arms, he left the room to make the call. It was a dangerous thing he was doing for both of them, but the die had been cast and he couldn't turn back. Layla would be his, body and soul, and then he would let her go. She was a queen and royalty never ended up with the common man.

# Chapter Twelve

### *Layla*

They were words she'd never expected to hear. Arlo wanted to go out with her. She replayed their conversation several times over and over in her head on the way to the restaurant. It was a date. An honest to goodness date.

The Pier was a restaurant that was near the beach of Lake Genoa. It was packed with locals and tourists but Arlo's call had managed to snag them a prime table close to the beach yet still in the shade of the building. Apparently, the staff knew who they were or else Arlo had paid them well in advance because they were given the star treatment as soon as they walked in the door.

Her companion was the perfect gentlemen. The touch of his hand to her lower back as he guided her to the table left her legs tingling. Neither liked to sit facing the wall so he joined her on the same side.

"Do you come here often?" Taking the menu from the server, Layla asked for a glass of water.

"No, but I hear it's nice." It didn't take him long to decide as he placed the large list of options on the table.

"Where do you usually eat?" She just realized she didn't really know that much about Arlo's day to day life.

"Home, Firenza, or I grab something with one of the guys at a local bar."

"There's no sense in asking what you recommend then." It was a tossup between the sea bass and the salmon for her.

"I'm having the New York steak." Arlo leaner closer and draped one arm across the back of her chair. He still smelled fresh and clean from the shower.

"A meat and potatoes kind of guy?" She fidgeted with the hem of her dress while glancing around the room. It shouldn't be but the whole experience of being here, being on a date was just weird. If she were back in Chicago, she'd be at home working on charts and figures. All around her were people, normal people having a good time eating out with friends or family. A life so normal to others, yet so elusive to her.

From where they sat, they could see boats float up and dock. Their passengers laughed as they disembarked and walked toward the bar. All her life she thought she'd had it all. Money, security, and a future but there was so much else she'd missed. A private school and lessons of every kind did not prepare one for real life.

The waitress returned to take their order. She'd decided on the salmon and her date had the steak.

Conversation was light as both were unused to this new situation. Surprisingly it didn't seem odd, they were both alike and yet different. The silence was comforting instead of awkward, as if he was giving her time to think things out in her mind. What did one do when they finally got a shot at what they'd always wanted? It was hard to believe it was real. Going slow and easy was probably the best. Layla risked a glance his way. Yes, slow and easy was exactly what she wanted him to do.

The food was delicious and she'd cleared her plate in no time flat. When Arlo pulled her chair closer to his, her mind was a blur. So much for being the self-assured, strong business woman. He had her floating in the air above her chair with only a touch and a nod.

"Dessert?" Arlo whispered near her ear. His warm breath on her neck sent a shiver down her arm. "Are you cold? I'd give you my coat but I'm packing. You'll just have to sit closer." He put an arm around her to share his heat. It worked. The big man was a furnace.

"I'm fine. Do you want something?" Their heads were close and the urge to touch his scruffy jaw got the best of her. The first two fingers of her right hand traced along to his chin. He'd shaved this morning but his five o'clock shadow was sharp to the touch. His hand covered hers and he pulled it to rest on his thigh as the server returned.

"We'll have the cookies and cream. Two spoons," Arlo ordered. The waitress cleared their table and left.

"I never pictured you as a cookie kind of guy."

With her hand still covered firmly, she had to lean closer, which had her mostly across his firm, hard chest. A woman could get used to this.

"I have a huge sweet tooth." A grin cut across his mouth as a large dish of vanilla ice cream and chocolate chip cookies was placed between the two of them. He let go of her fingers and handed her a spoon. When she didn't take it, he put a scoop of ice cream on the utensil and placed it between her lips. It was sensual and sweet.

Layla closed her eyes, enjoying the sensation of the surgery goodness and the handsome man. After the first taste, she dug in eagerly. The plate was almost gone when Arlo's phone beeped.

He answered it, saying few words. From the expression on his face, it wasn't good news. "We'll be right there." Waving the server over, he asked for the bill. Their fun evening had come to an end.

She barely kept up in her heels as they rushed out of the place. A few heads turned their way with their hasty exit. "Where are we going?"

"You'll find out soon." Arlo opened the vehicle door and helped her in.

He soon joined her in the SUV and started it up. "They found the leak."

"Did they say who?" This was good news as far as she was concerned.

"Not sure, but we'll find out soon."

It was a surreal experience driving through the town of Genoa. The street was bursting with happy tourists even at this late hour. How she wished they could have stayed longer at The Pier and maybe walked along the lake. Maybe another night. She'd be spending a lot of time here now that she'd bought a business. It wasn't her intention but things were falling into place.

Soon the restaurants and shops were behind them. The vehicle slowed as they turned down a dirt road. There in the distance a large building, or what might have been a garage business at one time, stood. Several other vehicles were parked out front, Caponelli vehicles. Something big was going down and they'd find out soon what it was.

They parked and Layla was out before he could open the door for her. "Are you sure you want to go in?"

Her outside voice said yes but inwardly she was screaming no. Layla'd heard bits and pieces of what the family did to traitors but as the future head of the Rinaldi *famiglia*, she needed to be strong. Her palms started to sweat. Bruno always kept her out of sight of the blood and guts but things were going to get real, fast. It was time to buck up and get her head on straight.

"You look pale." Arlo put both hands on the tops of her shoulders. "Are you sure? Things can get messy in here but I can't leave you alone."

"I'm fine, just a little cold." He took off his jacket and put it around her. The two guns he had secured in a double holster would have caused quite a scene at the place they'd just left. Wrapping the jacket tighter around her, she inhaled his aftershave. This day had been emotional and draining and what would happen next was anyone's guess.

Again he placed his hand along her back and pressed her forward. Her legs felt like lead but she could do this. She'd run most areas of the business but this was different. Her role was always overseeing the books, taxes, and working with the employees at the clubs. If her gut was right, this would be getting your hands dirty with someone's blood.

The sun had set and the sky had turned to stunning shades of orange and red. Arlo knocked on the door and it was Jasper who let them in. It was even darker in the building and it took a moment for her eyes to adjust. There in the middle of the large area was a lone bright light hanging from the ceiling. Below the light, a man slumped in a metal chair, his hands tied behind his back.

"Who the fuck is that?" Arlo asked gruffly.

"Christopher." Jasper spoke up behind them. "I don't like this one bit. If it wasn't for him, we'd never have found Jackie. He was the tech guy who alerted us she'd been taken." He explained for Layla's sake.

Layla turned to face him. "Taken?"

"By Fedor's brother. I owe him her life." Jasper cursed and shoved his hands in his pockets.

"But if he was involved with the bombings, he also almost killed her. Almost killed all of us," Arlo pointed out. "Let's hope that's not the case."

It was warmer inside but it still didn't take off the chills going down her spine. Layla slipped her arms through the large jacket and pulled it closer. The weight of it gave her comfort and strength.

"Let's go see what's up." Arlo waited for Jasper to lock the door behind them.

As they neared the men in the darkened room,

Layla looked for familiar faces. It was just Roman and Dominic that were there. Surprisingly, she expected there to be more.

Roman nodded at her while Dominic remained focused on their captive.

"Who is this man?" She wanted to hear Roman's side of the story. Hopefully her voice hid her nerves.

"Christopher, one of the tech guys." Roman appeared relaxed except for the slight twitch in his jaw. The lack of blood on the man showed the hadn't had time to question him yet.

"Why is he here?" Although she asked the questions, Layla remained to the side of Arlo. This was not her territory and there was no need to show disrespect to anyone in the family by stepping up or on anyone's toes.

"To find out what he knows." Roman slowly started to circle the chair. "It seemed odd that the bombs exploded at the same time but yet killed no one who was targeted. We suspected from the beginning that this must be tied to someone on the inside. Someone that would know where everyone was at all times."

Christopher kept his face down but you could see he trembled. Layla glanced from man to man. All were emotionless and focused on the guy in the middle.

"The person had to know where everyone was but yet the bomb went off when we were all safely away. Why is that?" Roman stopped in front of the chair for a moment before starting to walk again. "I sent files on our employees' homes with these guys and the only one that drew a red flag was Christopher's." Layla briefly looked at Arlo and there was no emotion on his face. "We pay you very well, Chris, yet all your credit cards are charged to the max paying off routine purchases. Food, rent, car payments. Why is that?" He stopped in front of the chair again. "Why is that?" Roman shouted, his voice reverberating in the large chamber.

Christopher looked up and she could see a tear roll down his face. "I got into something I couldn't get out of. I'm so sorry." He sobbed. "So sorry."

"What did you get into?" Metal scraped on the cement floor as Roman pulled a chair up and took a seat facing the doomed man.

"I…I have…had…a girlfriend in Chicago. I was going to propose. Being stupid, I stopped at a casino on the way, thinking I could gamble a bit and hopefully get an even bigger ring." He sniffled a few times as he explained. "I'm not much of a gambler, don't even know that much about it, but I thought I would just stop for half an hour and call it good." Christopher's jaw lowered to his chest.

"And?" This time it was Dominic that asked.

"I don't remember," Christopher admitted and Dominic turned his head toward Arlo, his eyes wary.

"What do you mean you don't remember?" The captive remained quiet and Roman continued. "There's one and only one reason that you aren't bleeding all over the floor right now and that is because you've saved the lives of people in this family several times. Now spill or I'll be forced to have Arlo get out his tools." Everyone turned toward the man who could make anyone talk but still he remained emotionless. Layla looped her arm around his. A mob boss, male or female, was supposed to be strong but if she had to watch Arlo torture someone, she'd probably be sick.

# Chapter Thirteen

### *Arlo*

"Did you hear me?" Roman asked quietly but Chris looked up and nodded. His face pale and strained. "What happened next?"

They'd never met in person but he'd talked to Chris several times on the phone. The kid looked young but had had been an expert at his job.

"We don't have all day." Roman stood up and motioned Arlo over but the guy finally found his voice.

"Okay, okay." Chris bounced in the metal chair.

Usually he enjoyed the chance to make someone talk, to get information, but the thought of doing that in front of someone he cared about turned his stomach. Her father expected to her rule but Layla would need someone she could trust to handle this part of the operation. She wasn't an enforcer, never was, never would be. He thanked his lucky stars that Chris agreed to spill his guts.

His boss took a seat again. "Talk, we don't have

all night."

"Like I said, I went to the casino and I don't remember what happened after that."

A slap sounded in the room as Roman reached out and smacked Chris across the face.

"I'm serious," Christopher argued. "I played a few games. A waitress came up and offered me a free drink so I took it. After she brought it to me, I drank another, and that's the last thing I remember. I woke up in the presidential suite. My mouth was dry, my head was spinning, and when I checked out, I had a hundred thousand dollar plus tab." The guy was on the verge of crying as he looked up to the heavens. "I tried to argue about it but they threw me in a room. Roughed me up a bit and wouldn't let me leave. I said I would call the cops but then he showed up."

"Who showed up?" Layla asked beside him. The expression on Christopher's face showed shock that a woman was here but if he'd thought they would go easy on him, he was mistaken.

"Some Russian guy, said his name was Fedor something. I had no clue who he was but when he showed me a picture of my girlfriend on his phone, I knew it was much worse than I thought."

His voice was raspy and Layla asked for some water for the man but Roman declined the offer.

"Keep talking and then we'll get you some water." The cautionary stare his boss gave Layla spoke volumes. She was to remain quiet for the rest of the interrogation. No compassion, no forgiveness.

"Like I said, the guy said his name was Fedor

114

and he was the head of the Russian mob. The freakin' mob."

"You work for the mob, you dumbass," Dominic grumbled.

"That's different. You pay me. I do surveillance just like a security company."

"We are not a fucking security company. I make people disappear. Forever. Does that sound like a normal, run of the mill security organization?" Dominic added.

"No." He stared at the ground.

"No? And yet you double cross us?" Dom got in his face.

"They took my girlfriend. They drugged me and somehow got me into debt for well over a hundred thousand dollars. Then they jacked up the interest so much I was in for over half a million in just a few months."

"Why didn't you come to us?" This time Jasper got into the action. "We could have helped."

"Aren't you listening?" he cried. "They had my girlfriend. The one I was going to ask to marry me." Chris groaned and shook his head. "When I didn't make the first payment…" he choked, "they sent me a picture of her with a bloody eye. Her pretty face a mess and in tears. They said if I told anyone they would start sending me pieces of her body in the mail. A few days later, I received a finger. A fucking finger! I didn't know if it was hers or not, but I was terrified. I had to save her. Had to do something."

Layla gasped. Arlo put an arm around her and pulled her to his side. Her delicate perfume was out of place in the stench of sweat and decay in the old building. Her soft curves molded to his hard body, giving him comfort.

"I emptied my bank account and started charging and advancing on my credit cards but it was never enough. I'd lost everything but he wanted more. Said we could work something out. I had not a clue what he wanted from me. No one knew what I did, I told him I worked for a small tech company but he knew." His lower lip quivered. "He knew I worked for you."

"So, he asked for intel?" It was a question, but Roman probably knew the answer. They all did.

"Yes, places of shipments. A few unknown warehouses in Chicago. Some of Bruno's hang out spots."

"The hits we've had in the last few months." Jasper walked over and placed a hand on the kid's shoulder. Christopher had to be in his mid-twenties but he appeared as vulnerable as a teenager.

"Yes, but what he didn't know was that as I was feeding info to him, I was also feeding intel back to me. I had to find my girl."

"How did you get access to Bruno?" Layla had stiffened at the sound of her father's name so he asked the question for her.

"By monitoring Connie's phone. As Roman's mother-in-law, she is under our protection and supervision. That's how I knew where they were having dinner that night. I knew something was up so made up a fake threat to get them both back home."

"Did he have you check on Layla also?" Arlo

had to know.

"I didn't have access to her but yes, he did ask, numerous times."

"What is his interest in Layla besides the obvious?" She is a beautiful woman but the guy had to be a lunatic if he thought she'd marry him.

"I'm sure he wanted to use her for leverage and didn't think he could get to anyone else. His brother, Alexander, disappeared and I think he thought we had him and he wanted to trade the girl for his brother. Fedor kept asking questions about him but I said I knew nothing. I didn't let on that we had him."

Roman rose. "What makes you think we do?"

"Don't know for sure but with him asking and you having a scrambler near a safe house I put two and two together." Chris laid his head back.

"But you said nothing?" Arlo got back into the conversation.

"Correct."

"He could be lying," Dominic jumped in.

"I'm not or you'd all be dead," Chris declared.

"And why aren't we all dead?" Their boss locked his hands behind his back and stared down at their captive.

"Like I said, I was monitoring all their info also. I didn't know about the bomb until about twenty minutes before. I love my girlfriend but I couldn't let you all die. I made a call to Bruno that he was needed at home, but I guess he was feeling unwell anyway. I also sent a warning to the boat that you had to come in due to the storm. There really was no storm warning. I wish I could have done more to save the people in the restaurant and on the ship but there was only so much I could do without raising suspicion."

"You said you loved your girlfriend; did you change your mind or did something happen to her?" Layla spoke up even though she'd been warned not to. Leave it to her to bring up something that he'd missed.

"I had to find a way out so I went even deeper into their intel. I found her on their payroll. It was all a set up. The woman I wanted to marry was a plant and I'm one hundred percent sure I was drugged at the casino. I was going to come forward with everything but I needed more time to get everything documented. You can check my files. Even if you killed me before hearing my story, I wanted you to know the truth. I tried my best to do what was right but…I was in over my head. Clearly. I'm just a stupid IT nerd that had a chick way hotter than I could have even imagined. It seemed too good to be true and it was." Chris was void of feeling and expression. The man appeared lost and to the point where he really didn't give a damn anymore.

"There's no love lost between Fedor and his brother, why does he want him back?" Arlo had wondered that ever since they'd captured him so he was glad that Roman had brought up the subject.

"It's some kind of Russian family rule to keep brothers from killing each other. If one is found guilty of killing the other, they will be dethroned. If the oldest brother is proven to be incapable of overseeing things, the younger one will be the boss.

I suspect Fedor still needs him to secure his leadership. I found some emails that people were not happy with this brother's disappearance. They think Fedor may have been behind it."

"But Alex is one hundred percent crazy. He's psychotic." Arlo knew that first hand. He'd been in on his torture and the guy just didn't give. It was like he felt no pain or was in a trance.

"Maybe, maybe not." Christopher added. "There were rumors that Fedor caused that in his brother but not sure how, why, or if it was even true."

The men exchanged glances before gazing back to the man in the middle.

"What do we do now?" Dom started to pace. He had issues with being in enclosed areas for too long and the fact that he'd been involved in a fight to the death match in this very spot probably didn't help either.

Roman walked over to them. "Since this involves both our families, what are your thoughts?"

You could have knocked Arlo over with a toothpick. That Roman had asked Layla's opinion was huge. It showed great respect for her and her family.

"He said he had a file with all the info. I would check that out first to see if it is true. I would then see what all he has on Fedor. What they've done and what they're planning to do. I'm assuming you have Alexander?" Both Roman and Arlo nodded.

"He's crazy." Jasper joined the conversation. "We should kill him and be done with it."

"Maybe he isn't so crazy after all." Layla raised

a finger to her lips.

"What do you mean?" He could guess where she was headed but he wanted to hear it from her lips.

"What if Fedor drove him crazy so he could take over?"

"He took a girl and left her near dead by the side of the road." Alexander was a sore spot for Jasper and for good reason.

"Just a second." Roman pulled out his phone and wandered off to make a call.

"What was that about?" Dominic now joined the conversation.

"I don't know." Arlo didn't know what to make of it all.

"I still think we need to see the files this guy said he was leaving us and see what he has on the Russians," Layla insisted.

"I don't trust him," Dominic reiterated.

"We'd have to monitor him closely but he might be the only way to find out what's really going on and if what he says is true. The man did save all our lives." It was true. They could all be dead right now.

"Thanks again and sorry for calling so late." Roman finished his call and joined their small circle. "That was Ryan. I asked him if the Russian girl they found had any distinguishing marks."

"You mean the one that Alexander took, who worked in one of the brothels. The one he left for dead along the road," Arlo explained for Layla's benefit. When she tilted her head his way, he added, "She had a tattoo on her arm from one of their houses."

"Yes, that one. And guess what?" Roman smiled for the first time since they arrived. "She's missing a little finger."

# Chapter Fourteen

They talked little on the drive back to his place. He replayed everything that was said, and it was a good bet that she was doing the same. Even after he parked and opened her door, Layla remained still.

"Ready to go in?"

"Oh, right. Yeah." Gathering her purse, she got out of the car.

He took her arm and escorted her into his building. It was usually comforting and quiet but today it just seemed empty and cold. Maybe when this was over, he'd buy a house, something on the lake or in the country. Unfortunately, without Layla, it would be lonely as hell so he might as well stay here.

Layla stopped at the elevator and pushed the button. Something was clearly on her mind. The doors opened and they stepped inside. He didn't bother arguing about not using the stairs today. Not to mention they'd put extra security on the property since she'd moved in.

"I'd like to see this woman." She finally broke

the silence.

"What woman?"

"The Russian prostitute that Chris was involved with." He figured as much. "Do you know where she is?"

"She's in a private rehab facility. Her injuries were substantial, both physical and mental."

"I can't imagine what she went through." Layla placed a hand over her heart as the elevator stopped on their floor. "I want to talk to her. Get her side of the story."

"I'm pretty sure that can be arranged." Arlo opened the door and ushered her in. "I've not seen Alexander for a while, I'd like to give him another try as well."

"You mean torture him?" She tossed her purse on a chair and took a seat on the couch. "Maybe a different approach might work."

"As in?" Arlo loosened his tie and sat next to her. Probably closer than he should but the woman was so distracted, he could take her in his arms and kiss her and she probably wouldn't even notice.

"Play one brother against the other. Even if Fedor isn't doing something nefarious to him, we could make it seem like he did." Beauty and brains, that's what this woman was. She may not have the muscle but she had the guts.

"I'll set something up tomorrow. We'll go see both. How's that sound?" Arlo put his arm over the back of the couch and Layla leaned into him.

"That sounds great. What should we do now?" The way she wiggled her eyebrows there was no mistaking her intention. The player was back and the words she'd said to Madison replayed in his mind. He should be holding back but if she wanted to jump his bones, why not go for it. Being the honorable one sure wasn't getting him anywhere.

Jumping up, she grabbed his hand. "I want to dance."

"It's late, Lay, and we have a long day tomorrow. I really don't feel like going out."

She turned around and dug around for the phone in her purse. "We don't have to go anywhere." Plopping her phone in his iPod station, music poured through the room. A romantic and sultry tune.

"Come." Layla curled her finger at him.

"No, I'm good." He stayed where he was but that might have been a mistake. Layla flipped off her shoes and stepped into the middle of the room. She swayed her hips and danced around as if she were the only one there or was it just supposed to appear that way? At one point, she even rolled on the ground and back up in an amazing move that would cause anyone else to fall and get up with back pain.

He had no clue about dancing or what style she was doing but Layla was magic. He'd never seen anyone twist their body and shift to the music the way she did. Well, maybe on TV he had when he'd caught someone watching those dance reality shows but this was up close. Layla had missed her calling. She could have been a dancer, should have been a dancer. Not left to run clubs and whorehouses for her father.

The song ended way too fast. Throughout the dance, she'd had her eyes closed but now Layla was regarding him. "I'm sorry. When I hear music, it takes me over and I forget anything and everything."

"Wow, you're great. I've never seen anything like that."

"Thanks." Her cheeks were pink. Was it from the dancing or embarrassment?

"Where'd you learn to do that?" He motioned with his hand to the area on the floor where she'd maneuvered like a world class dancer.

"Many, many years of lessons." On bare feet, she strolled over to sit on the couch arm.

"It shows." The next song was equally as enticing.

"Join me." Rising, Layla held out her arms. "You know I love dancing with you."

"And how do I know that?" He slowly rose.

"Because I keep asking." She took his hands in hers and led him to where she'd just finished twirling to the music.

"But why me?" Putting his arms around her and pulling her close was why he did it, but what was her reasoning?

"Why not you?" She lay her head on his shoulder as they started to slowly waltz around his living room. "You're strong, handsome, smart."

"And that appeals to you?" It was a question that he didn't expect an answer to but he hoped she would. He needed to know why she'd teased him for years, only to want to reject him in the end. It made no sense.

"Everything about you appeals to me."

Her words cut deep. Not knowing if she talked

125

the truth or was just saying bullshit to get a rise out of him. "How can you say that?" Arlo stepped back and held her wrist in his hands.

"What?" She frowned and her forehead crinkled. "All I've ever wanted was for you to like me."

"Why?" He tightened the hold on her wrists as she tightened the hold on his heart.

"Because it would be real." Her gaze fell to the floor and her lower lip quivered.

"I don't know what you mean." Arlo let go of her, turned off the music, and dragged her to the couch. "Spit it out. I've had enough of this BS. You tease me and yet I can't for the life of me figure out why."

"It's simple." The woman sat so close it was like she was sitting on his leg.

"Not to me. Spill." His patience at its end.

"My sweet sixteen." She entwined her fingers and placed them in her lap.

"Go on."

"I didn't want to go through with it," she admitted.

"The party? Why? I thought all girls loved that shit."

"Not if they don't have a mother."

He took a deep breath and let it out slowly. What did he know about having a mother? He'd lost his at an early age as well. His father was a hard man. A hard drinker, a hard womanizer, and a risk taker. Everything Arlo swore he'd never be.

For a girl it was probably different. Everything he still needed to know, he'd learned at Roman's side. They went through the same things at the same time. Mob and non-mob related. Mr. Caponelli never ran prostitutes but when he felt it was time for Roman and Arlo to be with members of the opposite sex, he called up Rinaldi and sent the two boys off to one of the man's houses. Bruno was there to greet them, maybe that was why the man never liked him but why wasn't the same said for Roman?

"I had no one to talk to about having a party. No one to show me how to wear makeup and dress pretty. No one to show me how to meet boys." Layla's admission brought him back to the present. "I hated the thought of the party. I cried for weeks, afraid that I would embarrass myself in front of everyone. Father thought it was crazy but finally gave in and bought me dance lessons. I was to do a first dance and hadn't a clue." She smiled for the first time in hours. "That was where I learned to love dancing. I took years of ballet, jazz, tap, belly dancing. You name it, and I wanted to learn how to do it. I may never be good enough to run the family but when I stepped on the dance floor, or put on my shoes, I was good at something."

"I think you are good at many things." He touched a fingertip to her chin and turned her jaw his way. "But it still doesn't explain why you wanted to dance with me."

"I knew many boys there were clamoring for me to pick them. Even Roman was expecting to be among the chosen ones. And why? Because they liked me? Hell no. I was just an end to a means. A small step on the climb to the top to get into my dad's graces. You didn't care about impressing anyone. When I talked to you out on the porch, you didn't even know who I was, yet you were nice to me anyway."

"Why wouldn't I be nice?" His father may have been an asshole but his mom had taught him manners.

"I saw the way those girls treated you when you asked them to dance. It was then that I knew you were the one to pick. When I threatened to run into the lake, you came after me. You could have walked away and said to hell with the drama but no, you were my hero."

"I was no such thing." He turned away and crossed his arms in front of his chest.

This time she put a finger to his jaw and turned his face her way. "You came into my life when I needed someone and I never forgot it. I never will forget it."

"Why does your father feel the way he does about me? He hates that I'm with you."

"I really don't know but I think he always wanted me to marry someone in the organization and not a rival family even though he tried to set me up with Roman."

"I heard you with Madison this morning." It was time to clear the air about everything. "You said you were just using me and then you'd marry whoever your father wanted you to. Why would you want to do that after what you just said?"

"I'm sorry you heard that but I promise, you only heard part of it. I was joking. It's always been you. I would never marry anyone that I didn't love, that ship has sailed." Layla drew up her skirt and straddled his lap. Framing his face with her hands, she stared straight into his eyes. "You're the one I want, the one I've always wanted and waited for. If you don't believe me, call up Madison and she'll repeat what I said. You, Arlo, you're mine. Always have been, always will be, and I want to be yours."

He groaned and his forehead touched hers. Could he trust her, believe her? God if only it was true. He couldn't just love her and leave her. When her lips touched his, it was too late. Layla Rinaldi may have bewitched him but he was doomed either way. He couldn't just love her and leave her. His arms pulled her close. The weight of her breasts pressed firm and full against his chest. She tasted of chocolate and mint, his new favorite flavor.

It was a battle of wills, his tongue doing a delicate dance with hers. She may know more on the dance floor than him but in the bedroom, he would be king. Her fingers threaded through his hair and she was breathing hard.

When they finally came up for air, her lips were red and swollen. "Don't turn me away again. I don't want to sleep another night in that bed alone." He should say no and run for the hills. This wouldn't end well. It couldn't, they were from two different worlds, two different stations in life. Call him weak but he couldn't take it anymore.

"I will never turn you away. You will always have a place with me. In my home, in my heart, in my bed. If this isn't a game, say so now, because if we make love, you're mine forever." He had to make that clear. The Caponelli men, whether blood or family, were fiercely protective and when they fell it was for life.

"Arlo, I'm not chasing you anymore, you have me right where I want to be. Make me yours and I'll be with you forever."

# Chapter Fifteen

## *Layla*

She held her breath waiting for his response. Didn't he believe her? It was now or never. Putting one's heart on the line was never easy but it had to be done. Some guys just didn't get it but she'd been hammering it into his head for years. Why had she made that stupid joke when she was with Maddy?

Maybe it'd been a mistake to be so forward, some men didn't like that, but Arlo always respected her no matter what. He was a real man and wouldn't back down or feel insecure about simple flirting. No, he didn't want his heart broken. Maybe if she'd had a mother to teach her subtlety and social graces, she could've gone about things differently but that wasn't to be.

It all boiled down to whether he cared for her or not. The seconds felt like minutes, the minutes felt like hours, yet the time they spent staring into each other's eyes was just a brief speck in time. If he turned her away, she'd go back to Chicago and never return. Lead a life of dance with no purpose or joy. Sure, they say time heals all wounds but, her all has always been about him. Ever since she was sweet sixteen and never been kissed. When Arlo kissed her, it was heaven on earth. Sun on a cloudy day. Feast after a famine. Something that couldn't be replaced.

He said nothing and Layla died a little inside. Edging off his lap, she stopped when he took hold of her.

"Where are you going?" His voice was raspy and deep.

"It's clear you don't want me." She bit her lip to keep from crying out.

"No, that's not true. I just wanted to enjoy having you in my arms for a moment longer." His palm cupped her cheek. Tears threatened to fall. She'd given it her all but he'd not given her an answer. "Before we go to the bedroom. Together."

Her mouth dropped opened and her heart soared. Layla wrapped her arms around his neck, tears streaming down her face. It was as if they were the only two people in the universe and that was okay with her.

Arlo pulled her away and framed her face in his hands. "Why the tears?" His thumb caressed her cheek.

"Sorry, I'm just emotional and very happy." Using the back of her hand, she tried to wipe the moisture away. "It's just finally getting something that I've wished for, dreamed for, for so long."

"I hope I don't disappoint." He lowered his hands to massage her shoulders. She melted

132

whenever he touched her and this was just the beginning.

"Nothing you could do would disappoint me except if you were to leave me."

"The only reason I would ever leave would be to save you. I'd give my life for yours." He dropped a kiss to her nose and the tears fell again. Arlo was the quiet man, the one who never shared his feelings, and yet he was baring his soul to her right now. It was the most intimate thing she'd ever experienced.

"And I for you. Never forget that. Never," she stressed and then pressed her lips to his. His arms pulled her hard to his chest. Still straddling his lap, her legs were tight against his. Her pelvis pressed up against Arlo's so much so she could feel how much he wanted her. It was too much, yet not enough. He tasted of coffee and sweets. Somewhere in the last few hours, he'd managed to snag a treat with cinnamon in it. She could taste it on his tongue. Maddy said he loved sugar and in the morning, she'd make him something sweet. Her mind was abuzz with too many things, too much sensory overload, and yet the only thing that mattered was Arlo. He was finally and truly all hers.

Not breaking the kiss, her man stood up, taking her with him. They briefly stopped at a wall, just long enough for Arlo to drop kisses along her neck and get a good hold of her ass. Then they were on the move again, only to spin a few times before making it to the bedroom. It was a simple gesture that imitated the dance she'd just done for him. He warmed her heart and her body.

When they entered the bedroom, nerves hit. As much as she wanted this, she didn't want to disappoint him. Layla was anything but experienced. Her time away from the social constraints of the family were limited. Her virginity was wasted on a one-night stand too many years ago to count when it should have been given to the one she loved. Too late to worry about that now.

Arlo gently tossed her on the soft bed. The down pillows and comforter felt like she'd landed on a cloud. Her man rolled up his sleeves and gave her a sexy smirk before hurling his tie over the back of a chair. Funny how at certain times, a person slows down enough to take in minor details you might not have noticed before. The dark hairs on his forearms, a large watch, the two rings he wore but she never thought to ask the meaning behind, and the pure look of adoration in his dark eyes. Butterflies in her stomach fluttered about and she curled one leg over the other before Arlo reached down and pulled it back.

"Everything all right?" He did the thing with his thumb again, caressing her ankle. Her pulse raced.

"Just nervous," she admitted.

"Nothing to be nervous about." He sat on the bed. "I would never make you do anything you don't want to do. You know that, right?" She nodded. "Are you on birth control?" Again, she nodded. "I'm clean. I don't sleep around and can't remember the last time I got laid. Once you came back into my life, no one else interested me. I don't have any condoms here, that's why I asked."

"I've never slept around either and I'm on the

pill." A few hours before she was a strong woman dealing with mob issues but now, she was thankful Arlo was asking the questions that needed to be asked and taking control of the situation. "They aren't always one hundred percent. What if I get pregnant?" She asked a question of her own.

"Then we'll just have to get married sooner that we plan." Layla's heart filled to capacity and the caressing of her ankle had moved to her calf. Her skin went back and forth between raised goosebumps and blazing heat. "Remember, anything you don't want me to do, just say no and I'll stop." Somehow, she didn't see that happening but Layla nodded anyway. He'd always been so kind and considerate of her and his patience with her now even more so. It was hard to imagine ever wanting to be with anyone else. There had never been anyone else.

"Take your dress off." She reached behind to undo the zipper and he helped to pull it off. Thankfully she'd worn pretty panties today but then her love for lovely lingerie made that easy. The gleam in his eyes showed his appreciation for the skimpy red piece of lace. "Those also." When she reached for her thong, his fingers replaced hers as he easily slid them down her legs, again leaving a trail of fire and ice along her skin as he went.

When Arlo started dropping kisses and nipping her legs with his mouth on the way up her thighs, her eyes nearly rolled back in her head. When he reached the center of her legs, they did. Her head fell to the side, her chest rose, and her legs quivered.

She placed her hands on his head and ran her fingers through his hair. It was thick yet soft. As he licked, sucked, and cherished her with his mouth, it was miraculous. Like a dream come true. It had come true. She was here, in this moment, in this bed with Arlo. A new sensation she'd never experienced before. It was intense, mind-blowing, and about to be over way too quickly. When Arlo took her little nub between his teeth and sucked, her head almost exploded. Stars flew and bombs went off. Collapsing into the fluffy comforter, a moan escaped her lips. Contentment, bliss, every word of joy she could think of fluttered through her mind.

"Hey, beautiful." Arlo leaned forward, his warm body covering her. He kissed her lips. The scent and taste of her arousal was all over his mouth. Layla pulled up the tail of his shirt and explored his back. Warm skin over hard muscle. What the rest of him must be like!

When he lifted his head and gazed into her eyes, his looked almost blue or was it hazel? They'd changed or maybe it was just her seeing him in a whole different light. "That was wonderful."

"That's just the beginning." A chill surrounded her when he got off the bed and she hugged herself. "Here, lift up so you can get under the covers." She snuggled in the warmth and turned onto her side as Arlo started to unbutton his shirt. It was like unwrapping a present, or at least in her mind it was. A gift she'd wanted and waited for since her sixteenth birthday, although at the time, she'd have been happy with just another dance or maybe a kiss. This was worth the wait and so much more.

As Arlo shed his shirt, every detail of his body came into view. He'd always been a large man, but the last few years he'd shed some pounds. Become leaner and stronger. His arms were muscular and his stomach cut and defined. It also showed the scars of wars and conflict. Someday she would get the story behind every welt and wound. He was beautiful in her eyes, flaws and all. Shoes, pants, and socks hit the floor before he joined her in bed.

He pulled his briefs off and again she was wrapped in the embrace of this amazing man, her man, and she would never get tired of saying it. How she wished she could have seen all of him before he got into bed but from the size and weight of his hard length pressed against her, it was probably a good thing. She had enough anxiety flowing through her veins right now to worry about anything else but dammit he was huge. Everything about him was.

"I don't want to wait any longer to make you mine." Arlo brushed the hair from her face and she nodded as he maneuvered again between her legs. This time it would be forever. He was making her his, marking her as his. His gaze never left hers as he entered her slowly, ever so slowly. The man had the will and patience of a saint. He was so gentle with her for their first time. After tonight, chances were good they'd be doing every position, in every place, but he clearly wanted this to be special for her. "All right?" Again, the caring lover, he kissed her lips.

"Yes." Tears threatened but she kept them at bay. Happiness poured over her. Dancing with him was her favorite thing until now, this…was off the charts. When he began to move, her whole world shifted. This was the start of the rest of her life. His thrusts brought her closer and closer to the edge again. Her gasps sounded in the room as he hit her sweet spot. Layla's ears burned and her face flushed. Her climax hit as pleasure rolled over and over her before falling back to earth. Arlo groaned and then joined her in their afterglow. His lips dropped kisses on the tip of her nose and each cheek. It was as if his eyes were seeing her soul and it belonged to him.

He rolled over, bringing her to his side. Resting her head on his hairy, roughened chest, the pounding of his heart matched hers. It hurt that Arlo had always thought he wasn't a high enough rank for her. Well, if he thought of her as queen, she knew he was her king.

# Chapter Sixteen

So much for getting up and making breakfast. As Layla finally crawled out of bed, she realized she'd be lucky if she could walk straight. Throwing on Arlo's abandoned dress shirt, she stretched and purred like a cat. They'd made love four times last night, exhaustion and elation were battling it out to see who might win. Finally making it to the bathroom, a new woman appeared in the mirror staring back at her. One that looked sexy, satisfied, and totally in love. Freshening up, she wobbled back to the bedroom. Muscles she never knew she had ached but in a good way.

"Coffee?" Arlo leaned against the wall, the grin on his face making him appear years younger. He was bare chested and wearing a pair of grey sweat pants low on his hips.

"A man after my heart." She drew the mug to her nose and inhaled. Bliss in a cup.

"I thought I already had it," he teased.

"That's right, you do." Setting the cup on a table, Layla strolled over and wrapped her arms around his waist. Looking up, she fluttered her fingers across his chest hair. They were both sweaty and smelled like sex. "We need a shower. Care to join me?"

"I'd love to but I have something to tell you first."

Layla raised an eyebrow.

"I have an appointment for you to meet with Tonya today."

"Who?"

"The Russian girl. I found out her name and the place she's recuperating at. If we can be there by ten, you can talk to her."

"Then we better get cleaned up." She grabbed his hand and pulled him toward the bathroom.

\*\*\*

As were most medical buildings in Genoa, the rehab center was fairly new and up to date. A lot of the improvements had been funded by the Caponelli family as they'd made numerous investments and donations to the town.

Layla decided on a simple sundress and light-colored wedges. It was peach with white flowers. She'd always loved pretty things but for some reason, she felt especially girly and feminine today. Layla placed her hand on Arlo's leg and he covered it with his. His strength eased some of the edge that she'd always felt the need to present to others. They complemented each other well, and during the journey over each had discussed different ways to approach the situation.

For this visit, empathy would hopefully get a better response than coming off too fierce. It was important to find out if Christopher could be trusted and this the first connection anyone had with the woman that they'd found. Arlo parked the SUV near the door and took her hand in his. When she turned his way, he greeted her with a kiss.

"I haven't met Tonya in person but I heard it was pretty bad, so be prepared," he warned while rubbing his thumb on her skin. In the middle of their many lovemaking sessions last night, she'd shared one of her fears. The sight of blood left her light headed, something that would be seen as a weakness for a leader. So far, Layla'd hidden it well, but knowing the poor woman would be missing a finger and who knows what else left her hands shaking.

"I will. Thanks." Crossing her arms in front of her chest, she waited for Arlo to get out and go around to open the door for her. Her man reached for her arm and held it as they walked. They were supposed to pretend to be a couple and now they officially were. Reaching the front of the building, he moved his hand to her lower back and guided her through the front entrance.

A member of the staff greeted them. "Can I help you?"

"We're here to see Tonya Yerkhov." Layla studied the place as Arlo spoke with the administrator, at least that was what her name tag stated she was. Her name, Sandra Evans, was in bold letters above her title.

The friendly expression on the woman's face

141

dropped and was replaced with a guarded one. "And you know this person how?"

"We're here representing the Caponellis," Arlo volunteered. They'd personally been paying all her healthcare since the woman had arrived there.

"Of course, but I will need to follow protocol and give them a call. I need your names and photo IDs please." They each gave her their driver's licenses. "Thanks, I'll make a call and get back to you shortly. Please take a seat while you wait." Miss Evans pointed to a small waiting room. The flat screen above a fireplace played the weather channel.

"We will. Thank you." Arlo entwined his fingers with hers and led her over to a loveseat.

"Did you know about their policies?" This was obviously more than your average rehabilitation center. It was a maximum-security facility.

He took a seat against the wall and patted the seat beside him. "I've never been here before so I had no idea, but it makes sense. She's the victim of a crime. Tonya needs quiet, care, and above all, to feel safe."

A few minutes later, Miss Evans returned. "I just talked to Mr. Caponelli and he said you were here on his behalf. Please follow me and I will escort you to Miss Yerkhov's room."

They were buzzed through a metal door and into the patient area. A common room held a few people chatting over mugs of coffee. Several rooms they passed had open doors. Patients were in their beds, some reading, resting, or watching TV. Applause for what sounded like a game show echoed as they passed one.

Sandra placed her hand on the door of the last room. "Tonya's made great progress since she's been with us but there is still a long way to go."

"What were the extent of her injuries?" Layla wanted to prepare herself for the worst.

"Mr. Caponelli gave me permission to share that information with you. She was tortured. Bones were broken, she was burned and cut, including missing a finger. Her body will heal but it's her mental state that concerns us most."

"That bastard," Arlo grumbled. "Was she sexually assaulted?"

"Fortunately, no. The woman is in a deep depression, as is expected after what she's been through. Hopefully your visit will improve that and give her something else to think about."

"Yes, let's hope." Layla nodded, her heart in her throat. "Thank you, Miss Evans." How horrible! If she was working for the Russians, why did they do this to her? Arlo had filled her in on what Alexander had said. That the woman was a favorite of his brother's and that's why he took her. Revenge against Fedor. He'd also said that their captive showed no remorse and then went on to take Jackie. It didn't make sense as far as she was concerned. If it was done to hurt his brother, why pick someone else right off the street?

Sandra knocked lightly on the door and a woman's voice answered from the room. The administrator opened it and took a step inside. "Tonya, you have visitors."

Sitting in a chair by the window was a small

blonde woman, in her lap was a book. Her hair curtained her facial features, but her eyes widened when they landed on Arlo. "Don't worry, dear, these people are with the Caponellis. They're just here to see how you're doing. Is it okay that they sit with you? Would you like to go out in the common area?"

Tonya's eyes fluttered back and forth between the three before finally settling on Layla. Her head slowly nodded up and down.

"Here, or out there?" Sandra asked again.

The young woman's mouth twitched. "Here." She untucked her feet from under her and placed them on the floor.

"I'll leave the door open and check back in a bit," Miss Evans said to Tonya before leaving.

An awkward silence settled in the room before Layla spoke. "Hi, I'm Layla." Ambling forward with her hand out, she stood before her but there was no response from the young lady. Letting her arm fall to her side, she tried again. "Is it okay if I take a seat on the bed?" Arlo remained by the door.

Tonya slowly nodded and set her book on the window sill. It appeared to be a paperback romance. Grabbing a nearby pillow, she placed it in front of her chest. Again, her eyes darted to the large man leaning against the doorway. Up close the traces of her injuries were more apparent. It had been months but scars and discoloration still marred her face. Her nose and perhaps even her jaw had been broken.

"I'm sorry for what you went through. Like I said, my name is Layla Rinaldi, and this is Arlo Brunetti, he works very closely with Mr. Caponelli.

144

Roman's wife is my half-sister."

Tonya's shoulders visibly relaxed. "We are here to try and help. Are you feeling better? Is there anything we can get for you?" Layla remembered the nearby paperback. "More books perhaps? Any favorite kinds of chocolate or food we can get you?"

The woman shook her head. "What is it that you want to know?" Tonya spoke with a distinct Russian accent. "The Caponellis have been paying my bills so I figured it would come with a price."

"No price, but we do have questions." Arlo stepped away from the wall. "We know you worked at one of the whorehouses owned by the Bratva. How did you come to be here?"

"You know the answer. That pig, Alexander, took me and..." Her voice cracked. "Did horrible things and tossed me by the side of the road."

"Why you?" Layla asked but there was no response.

"Alexander said you were a favorite of his brother's. Did he visit you often at the brothel?" Arlo gave it a try and when she remained silent added, "Were you there willingly?"

Tonya took a deep breath. "Hell no. I was drugged at a club while on holiday in France. A few days later I woke up in what I later found out was Chicago. They made me work in the house but as a housekeeper, cleaning the rooms. Fedor said if I didn't want to end up as a whore, I needed to do work for him. Do as he said."

"What kind of work?" he asked.

"My English was good so he said he had a job

for me. Told me if I could make someone fall for me, a man. Then I could go free."

"And did you?" Layla crossed one leg over the other.

"I'd have done anything to go home and not have to be forced into prostitution."

"Who was the man?" Arlo inched closer and took a seat in a nearby chair.

"His name was Christopher. He was an IT specialist that I met at a bar. Somehow they knew he would be there." A slight blush crossed her face. "He was nice and kind to me. We began dating. The more time we spent together the more I liked him. We fell in love. It was no longer just a job to me." Her blue eyes watered. "I really cared for him and hoped he could get me out of there. Have a future together."

"What happened next?" Layla knew but they needed to know for sure.

"They threatened me to get information from him. At that point I didn't want to but they said they would hurt him. It made me sick. I knew what they'd do to me so I couldn't bear to have them hurt him." A tear rolled down her cheek.

Layla wanted to give the girl comfort but they needed to know more. "Why did Alexander take you, he said you were his brother's favorite but yet you were helping them."

"I hated Fedor, and no, I never slept with him or anyone there. It was the one promise he kept to me in exchange for doing what I was told. It was just an excuse he told everyone so they would leave me alone. I didn't really know Alex. I used to feel sorry for him. It was rumored that he was being drugged or poisoned by Fedor. I'm not sure which."

Layla's eyes locked on Arlo. "Poisoned?"

"Yes, the girls used to say he was kind and that Fedor was a beast. That Fedor wanted to run the business in the worst way and the only way was to get rid of his older brother. Alex changed and became crazy, and…I can't think of the word. Part…pare…paranoid." She snapped her fingers. "That's what it is, paranoid. That everyone was out to get him. When he'd visit the house, women would be terrified he'd want to be with them because he was so mean. Brutal. But he hadn't been that way before." Tonya pulled the pillow tighter to her body. "Right before he took me, Fedor cut off my finger and sent it to Christopher. They were blackmailing him for information on his employer. They're both monsters," she cried.

"Do you know who Christopher worked for?" Layla asked and Tonya shook her head.

"No, I didn't ask questions but I did what they told me to. Before I was taken, Fedor told me he was done with me. He also said he was done with Chris and that he was going to kill him. I tried to escape and it was then that Alex took me." The pillow fell to the floor and Tonya rested her elbows on her knees. "I'm responsible for his death. He was a good man and it was my actions that killed him. I just wanted to be free, not fall in love with someone. I deserve what was done to me. This was all my fault."

"No, no, you didn't. None of this is your fault." Layla inched closer to the edge of the bed and rested her hand on Tonya's shoulder. "And I have good news for you. Your Christopher is alive."

# Chapter Seventeen

## *Arlo*

Tonya was full of questions and they tried to fill her in as much as they could. As a patient there, she'd had no contact with the outside world and hadn't since being admitted. Now that she knew her lover was safe and sound, Tonya's spirits improved by leaps and bounds.

Layla promised to come visit her again and she managed to find out a few of the girl's favorite things. Knowing Layla's kind heart, she would soon be returning with a care basket filled with goodies.

"Where to now?" Back in the vehicle, his beautiful companion asked while typing on her phone.

"We're meeting the family doctor at the safe house. She has some new insight on Alexander that she wants to discuss with us."

"Insight?" She put away her phone and looked his way.

"Apparently, he's had some drastic changes in

behavior the last month." The guy couldn't get any worse so it was hard to guess what this could mean.

"Changes?" Layla crossed her legs and his eyes naturally fell to her long limbs. Damn, she was beautiful. Every day he spent with her, he felt his heart grow larger as it filled with love. Sure, their time together had been brief, but it had been years in coming.

"Yeah, that's what they said. I'm curious to hear what she has to say. Anything to get some insight into what's going on."

"What's your gut tell you?" Layla flipped the visor down and flicked a piece of fuzz from her dress.

"My gut tells me something happened between the brothers. Alexander ruled after their father's death but Fedor took over. It was after that, that the attacks on the Rinaldi and Caponelli territories started to happen." Before that there was somewhat of a truce between the families and the Bratva but that changed dramatically in the last few months. Not to mention what happened with them trying to eliminate everyone this past weekend.

It took a little longer than usual to get through town, the tourist season was in full force. Parking downtown was pretty much non-existent. The normal ten-minute drive took over twenty. When they reached the safe house, Arlo parked in the driveway next to the doctor's car. Just like Valentina was the Caponellis' full time lawyer, the family also had an MD on call at all times.

The curtains inside the house moved as Alexander's guard checked them out. "Let's go."

"Is Alex under control?" Layla reached for her purse and put it in her lap.

"Don't worry, he's under glass." That got him a confused look from the woman next to him but she didn't ask anything more. Arlo got out of the car and surveyed the area. It was a work day and this was a working-class neighborhood so very few cars or people were around.

"Under glass, huh?" she asked when he opened her door and helped her out.

"You'll see."

Oscar greeted them at the side door and quickly closed and locked it behind them. "What's new, Ar?"

"Not much, O, how about yourself?" Oscar had been working with them for a few months and so far, seemed to work out well. He was becoming a loyal and trusted member of the family.

"Good, I like when the Doc visits. She's a looker." Oscar nodded to Layla. "Hi, ma'am."

"Oscar, Layla. Layla, Oscar." Arlo made introductions. "What's going on with the prisoner?"

"I'm not sure but there's been a change in him. He's almost normal. The Doc's been doing tests and trying different drugs. It seems to be working, at least it seems so to me."

"How so?" Layla spoke up.

"When he first got here, the guy acted like he was on something. Breathing hard, but never seemed to notice things. Like he was stoned. I once watched him repeatedly slam his head against the wall and never feel a thing. The other day, he stubbed his toe on the edge of a table and hopped around like he'd broken his leg."

That was interesting. "What else?"

"He was never sociable. Never noticed who was here or seemed to care. Now he greets us, thanks us for the meals, and even seems to want to talk. It's fuc—I mean, freakin' weird." He glanced at Layla. "Sorry about the language."

"I've heard worse but thank you." Layla put the man at ease.

"Well, the Doc's almost done." Oscar barely got out before a woman who looked to be around thirty came into the room.

"Hello, Carrie," Arlo greeted.

"Arlo, you're looking well." She was a medium height woman with a slight frame and straight dark hair.

"Doing well. I'd like you to meet Layla Rinaldi." They exchanged greetings and Carrie invited them to take a seat.

"I alerted Roman of the modifications in the patient's behavior. It's my diagnosis that Alexander has been suffering with undiagnosed paranoid schizophrenia for years. He has the right family history, an older father, drug use in his teens, and both he and his brother were born premature." She leafed through a file that had been lying on the table. "Thanks to your tech guys, we were able to get all his medical records. From interviewing Alex, it's my suspicion that he was being fed various drugs in low doses, which increased the paranoia. Either in food or drink, it doesn't really matter. Who knows, his brother may have been putting thoughts in his mind as well to encourage his erratic

152

behavior. Alex was psychotic when he first came here, he had no empathy and felt no pain or remorse for what he'd done. I've been monitoring his blood work. I wasn't able to identify everything that was in his system, but there were traces of LSD, which Alex denies taking. I've been giving him clozapine. It helps with paranoia and seems to be working. He's actually behaving quite normal now, or what you would consider normal for those in his profession."

Arlo and Layla exchanged glances.

"You don't think he's acting?" Layla rested a finger on her chin.

"No one's that good." She laughed. "I heard what you did to him, Arlo, and the guy didn't budge. The lack of response can only be attributed to some kind of nerve or a mental issue. He flinched when I drew blood last week, that's the first time he's done that and we've been poking him ever since he's been here."

"Interesting." Arlo mulled it over in his head. It was starting to make sense. Fedor wanted control but couldn't kill his brother and remain the head of the Bratva. He had to eliminate him some other way. His intent was probably to have him declared insane but the guy took off with Tonya first. "Can we see him?"

"Of course." Carrie stood up. "Please follow me."

Arlo hadn't been there many times. He'd worked Alexander over pretty good right after they'd saved Jackie, but he hadn't touched him since.

Once they got into the main part of the house,

Layla could clearly see what he meant when he'd said Alex was under glass, or technically behind glass. The place was one big room, divided by heavy plated panels, the guards on one side and Alexander on the other. It was almost like a scene from *Silence of the Lambs*. There was a heavy door in the middle where they could go back and forth. If the doctor needed to go in, the guards could belt Alexander's arms and legs to a chair so she could work on him.

Alexander was sitting in a chair watching TV. When he turned toward his visitors, he picked up the remote and turned it off. Rising, the tall man approached the glass. "I know you." His attention was on Layla and she stepped closer to the glass. Alexander snapped his fingers a few times. "You are...hmm." He frowned and then smiled. "I got it. You're Layla Rinaldi."

"And how do you know me?" She placed one hand on the divider. "I don't believe we've met before."

"We haven't, but once my brother saw a photo of you in the newspaper. He was obsessed after that. Said he was going to marry you and rule the city."

Arlo noticed her face turn red.

"I thought you ruled the city," she responded.

"Ha, we ruled together but then he wanted more. Didn't want my say in anything anymore."

"So, why didn't you take him out?" Arlo dug for more info.

"He's my brother and it's part of the code. If I kill him, I lose everything."

"So, you took his girlfriend instead?"

154

Alex rubbed his hand over his face. "The past year's a bit fuzzy. He said he was trying to protect me, that others wanted me dead. That Tonya wanted to destroy me even. I don't remember all that was said. Just that I had so much rage and nowhere to get rid of it." The man exhaled and took a seat at the small table in his room. "You have to tell me. Is she okay?"

"Who?" Arlo wondered.

"Tonya. I have these visions of what I did to her and I can't imagine doing that. It's like a dream."

This was not at all the man he'd captured months ago, about to do unspeakable things to Jackie as she was strapped to a table. "You torture a woman, beat her almost beyond recognition, and now you want to know how she is?" Arlo let him have it. "How do you think she is?"

"That wasn't me. It couldn't have been. I'm no saint, I admit it. I'm in the Russian mob for fuck's sake. I've killed people but I'd never hurt a woman before and they said I tried to do that to another one." He shook his head. "I don't remember that. I would never do that."

Arlo locked eyes with the doctor and she raised an eyebrow. Alexander was either a really good actor or what he said was true. The combination of an untreated mental illness and doping had created a monster. "You did. I was there when we rescued her."

Alexander stood up and paced back and forth, seeming to weigh his options. Finally, he stopped and sat down. Putting his elbows on his knees, he placed his face in his hands. "Fedor did this to me.

My own fucking brother poisoned me with drugs to take control." Slowly he looked up and said, "I have a feeling you are telling me this so that I will do something for you? What do you want?"

"What do you need to know?"

Arlo pulled out a chair, sat down, and tugged a little notepad from his pocket. "I want names and places."

"That I can't do." Alexander slumped back in the chair. "I can't betray the Bratva. They'll kill me."

"You have two choices." Arlo crossed his ankle on top of his knee. "You answer my questions and we might, just might, let you go so you can even the score with your brother and set things straight with the Bratva."

"And the other choice?" The man behind the glass chuckled.

"If you don't answer my questions, I'll kill you."

# Chapter Eighteen

### *Layla*

Arlo was silent on the way to her sister's. They'd stopped for some pizza for lunch and he'd spent most of the time on a burner phone with Roman. Things had been set in motion but what that was exactly, she wasn't sure yet. Being born in the family, she knew it wasn't good.

"Are you going to share what's going on?" she finally asked.

"In time. We're having a meeting once we get there. Your father will be involved as well."

"We're going to war." Her heart sank.

"We've been at war. It was declared the moment they blew up the boat. You know it did." Arlo's voice was flat and emotionless.

"I do, I just hoped it wouldn't come to this." So much for being a leader. All she wanted right now was to give up everything they had to keep the people she loved safe but that wasn't how things worked.

They halted at a stop sign and he leaned over to give her a kiss on the cheek. "It always comes to this. Last man standing wins."

Her head landed back on the head rest. More people would die soon and there wasn't a damn thing she could do about it. Madison had made it her goal to get more and more of Roman's business legit but his ties to her father had complicated things. Roman was bound by family and now blood to avenge both the attack on Bruno and at the wedding.

There was a pit in her stomach as they drove through the gates of the Caponelli estate. The yard was filled with vehicles, including the white van that Dominic drove. As soon as they stopped, she was out of the car. No need to wait for Arlo to open it, they were safe here and she couldn't sit idle any longer.

Walking fast, Arlo finally caught up with her as she put her finger to the doorbell. It was Jasper who opened it and waved them inside. The place was packed with men but she couldn't hear what they were saying. There was just static in her brain as she tried to process everything going on.

"Layla!" Maddy yelled as she came down the stairway. Her husband had her arm as they made their way down. As soon as they got to the bottom, her sister rushed to her side. Her face was pale and her skin clammy.

"Are you all right? You're as white as a ghost." Layla put her arms around her.

"Yes, yes. I'm fine." She nodded and then bit her lip.

"Are you sure? I can get you some water."

"No, no. I'm good."

"Gentlemen," Roman called out. "Meet me in the study. We have a lot to talk about." As the men funneled into the office, Arlo left her in Maddy's care and said he would speak with her when he knew more.

"Come into the kitchen." Madison looped her arm in Layla's and led the way. As soon as they entered the room, she could see Stephanie and Jackie nursing glasses of wine. "If I wasn't pregnant, I'd be having one of those. too." Maddy dropped her arm and walked over to the other two.

"Pour me one." Layla didn't wait for it to be offered. "And fill it to the top."

"I'm on it." Jackie rose and took another wine glass from the cabinet. She placed the goblet of Cabernet in front of one of the chairs at the counter and motioned for her to take a seat. "Have some cheese." Layla's gaze fell to the platter full of cheese and meat. It never failed to amaze her how people in Wisconsin pulled out a plate of cheese no matter what the occasion, whether it be wedding, birthday party, or pre-mob hit. The Asiago did look good though and she plopped a piece in her mouth.

"What do you think this means?" Jackie asked.

"I don't know everything but from the information they gathered from Alexander it appears they will strike one or two of the locations he mentioned. Tonight," Madison answered.

Jackie gasped and put a napkin to her lips. "Who's going?"

"Everyone, including Roman." That explained

the faintness of her complexion. They were expecting their first child. The pair should be picking out baby furniture, not dealing with the possibly of the father getting hurt or killed.

"Jasper, too?" the redhead asked. Jackie was the newest one to the family so this was going to be a shock for her to think of her man in harm's way.

"Everyone but a few guards. Dominic will stay." Madison seemed to have more of the details than anyone else.

Stephanie let out a deep breath. "I had hoped he wouldn't go. Dom thought they would need someone to scatter the phones and he usually doesn't get too involved in things. Just cleans up what needs to be."

"Scatter the phones?" Jackie glanced between the women.

"It's no secret that they think the phones are being traced and tracked. To throw them off, Dom will take Roman's, Jasper's, and Arlo's phones with him. He's going to go to a bar for as long as it takes for them to get to Chicago. He'll have a burner with him to keep up to date. Anyone monitoring them will think they are out for drinks. Every now and then he will pick one up and walk around the place so they are all in action," Maddy explained. "The guys will hit their targets and come right back. As soon as Dom gets the word, he'll be back here to let us know what's going on."

"I'm going to be sick. What if someone gets killed?" Jackie leaned her head on Layla's shoulder.

"We can only hope it will be the ones responsible for murdering all the innocent people in the restaurant and on the boat last weekend." Either way, someone was probably going to die tonight. Layla's eyes met Maddy's across the table. It was going to be a very, very long night.

The meeting went surprisingly fast. In no time at all, Roman came into the kitchen, followed closely by Jasper, Dom, and Arlo. They each went to their women to exchange words, hugs, kisses, and a few promises. Even though Dominic was staying behind, it was a hard situation for everyone. His job was vital to throw their trackers off their trail.

Shortly after, all the guys except Dom disappeared to change into all black. When they returned, they were heavily armed and wired for action. It was even more stressful knowing that Christopher was still handling the surveillance. He'd sworn his allegiance, and even though he knew Tonya was safe and sound, it still didn't ease her fears as far as Layla was concerned. Roman thought he could be trusted and he was the boss.

"Everyone ready?" Roman glanced from man to man. They either spoke out loud or nodded. The boss then went over and kissed Madison goodbye. Jasper did the same with Jackie. Layla witnessed it all happen as if it were just a dream. She couldn't look at Arlo. As long as she didn't, it wasn't real. Right? They'd waited too long to be together for this to break them apart. With her eyes trained on the floor, his shoes came into view. They were dark tennis shoes, all the reflector material blacked out. Funny what you notice when you're trying to block other things out.

He put both hands on her face and raised her

gaze to meet his. "Aren't you going to say goodbye?"

"No, because you'll be coming back soon. You have to." Tears streamed down her face.

"Don't worry, sweetheart. Not even death could keep me from your door." He tipped her chin up so she had to gaze into his eyes.

"There's been something I've wanted to tell you." Layla grabbed the lapel of his suit.

Arlo shook his head. "No, no. Don't you dare say that you love me or want to marry me or any of that shit. I can't bear to hear those words now. If you mean it, tell me when I least expect it. When I know without a doubt you mean it, and aren't just saying what I want to hear to make me feel better in case I don't come back."

"But…" Layla shook her head.

"No. You know how I feel about you but I still have a few issues about what I heard you say upstairs."

"Seriously? You know I was joking." Shaking her head, she continued, "This isn't the time to rehash this."

"That's exactly why I'm saying this. Don't make promises or say words that you might want to take back at a later date."

Her eyes focused on his, trying to read the meaning behind the words. In her heart she knew he cared about her but hearing it might just make everything worse. It would be something she'd never recover from if he didn't return.

"Layla, a word," Roman interrupted them. "Sorry, Arlo, but I need a moment with Layla."

Reluctantly Arlo nodded and released her. She followed him to the door as the girls led Madison to the living room.

"I need you to look after your sister," he said. The man had enough to worry about without having to think about her welfare.

"Of course. Always," she reassured.

"No, I mean if something happens to me, you move here and take care of her. I don't care about family honor or whatever, you put her first." He put his hands on the top of her shoulders.

"Yes, you don't need to ask. She's my family."

"Good." Roman kissed her cheek. "Thank you."

He turned to leave and Layla pulled him back. This time it was her that put two hands on his shoulders. "I want you to bring Arlo back. Bring all the men back."

"That's the plan."

She wrapped her arms around his waist and gave him a quick hug. "Be safe. That baby needs a father."

"I'll be back. We all will." Roman waved his arm. "Let's go, men. Dom, you know what to do."

They all followed with Arlo bringing up the rear. He stopped to embrace her again and drop a kiss to her forehead. "We'll be back soon."

All she could do was nod. A big lump had lodged in her throat, preventing her from saying any more. Layla leaned against the doorframe and watched the guys climb into a black SUV with Dominic in the driver's seat. They would be driving together to the bar. There another vehicle would be waiting to pick them up. Dom would stay there with

163

all their phones. The others would be going dark or using the burners.

She couldn't move until their taillights disappeared through the gates. It was going to be a very long night. The mission would hopefully be done by midnight. Closing the door, Layla took a deep breath and headed to the living room. Madison needed her and Jackie probably did also. Stephanie was the only one who would be breathing easy for the next few hours because her man was safe, but that didn't mean she wasn't feeling the stress surrounding the house.

When she entered the room, Stephanie was collecting everyone's order for some take out from Firenza. "I don't feel hungry." Madison was slumped in a chair.

"You have to eat. The baby needs food even if you don't." Her gaze met Stephanie's and she crossed her arms in front of her chest. It was going to be a long night and it would take the two of them to keep the mood up.

"I'll help you pick something out," Layla volunteered. "And then we're going to find a good movie to watch. I trust the guys. They're good fighters, they practice all the time, and they have good intel." She took a seat between Maddy and Jackie. "They will get through this and we will too." As much as she tried to comfort the rest, it wasn't doing much to calm herself.

Her heart was in her throat. She'd waited too long to make Arlo hers only to lose him. Putting her arms around each woman, Layla did something she'd not done in a very long time. Prayed.

# Chapter Nineteen

## *Arlo*

It felt like they were never going to get there. They told the women it would only be a quick in and out operation but things never went that smooth. Roman also didn't want to worry them. The plan was to have Dominic come back later, tell the women everything was fine, and hopefully they would then go to bed. Last thing anyone wanted was for Madison to be under stress.

The countryside zoomed by outside his window as they made their way to Chicago. Arlo rode shotgun while Oscar drove. Jasper and Roman coordinated things by phone in the backseat with the other soldiers on the ground. Rinaldi had offered up troops as well.

Whether or not to get the police involved was also being discussed. One of the spots they were hitting was the brothel Tonya had worked in. The women there were being held against their will, had been victims of trafficking, or both. It was decided that the authorities would be called in when everyone was out of there but the girls. They would be able to help them the most and hopefully get them the care they needed and back to their homes.

When they were all in place, they would strike. It would be fast and very painful. They were hitting Fedor where it hurt, all the places he made the most money.

The targets would be hit at the same time. Between the Rinaldis, Caponellis, and a few other Chicago families that hated the Russians as much as they did, it would be a major blow to his organization. The spots were a combination of offsite gambling dens, brothels, warehouses, and even a few bars they owned. That's why it would be a long night. They needed to wait until most of them were closed. Fedor may not care about innocent people's lives but they did.

Dominic would get back about midnight and let the ladies know they were all right. It was then that they would strike. Dom would make it clear they were not to call and that they would all talk in the morning.

It didn't sit well the way he'd left things with Layla. In a moment of weakness, he recalled what he'd heard Layla tell her sister and he let himself believe it again. Better that than second guess everything he did tonight and possibly get himself or someone else killed. Never before had he gone into battle concerned about leaving a loved one behind. Why? Because before there were none. It was a whole new experience for him and one that he battled with.

Their brief time together had been heaven. A dream that'd come true but was it just a dream? They were doomed from the get-go. Her father hated him for some reason. And what if some miracle happened, Layla and he did marry, her husband would rule the Rinaldi family with her. He'd never leave the Caponellis. They'd taken him in when he had no place left to go. They'd given him something he'd wanted for so long after his parents had died. The Caponellis had made him family.

After going through a drive-through along the way—even bad boys needed to eat—they drove through the gates of the Rinaldi mansion. He'd not been there since Roman and Madison's wedding. That was the night he'd danced with Layla again. The night that feelings had started to develop, and it wasn't just curiosity about what had happened to the beautiful sweet sixteen girl.

Bruno met them at the door. He was dressed in all black as well, which surprised him. The man must have planned on going along.

"Come in, gentlemen."

They followed Mr. Rinaldi to his office. Along the way, Arlo took notice of the elaborate paintings, crystal chandeliers, and endless rooms. When he'd been there before, he'd never paid much attention to his surroundings. The place was not only huge but practically dripping in cash. It was just another reason Layla and he were not destined to be together. He made good money, great actually. Never one for showy suits or cars, Arlo had invested well and spent little, but he was still no match for the wealth Layla's family had.

His mood darkened. It was time to get this operation on the road. As they entered his office, it became clear that Bruno had done his research as well. The guy may be up in years but he wasn't ready to give up the reins any time soon. There was a map on the desk showcasing the location they would hit.

"I have two teams here and here and here. They leave each night with bags of money. When we hit, we'll take the money and blow each place up. The warehouses will be raided and we have trucks lined up to take as much as we can before we blow them up. Your guys will take the brothels. Each place closes at two, so we still have some time."

Jasper pointed toward the location they would be going to on the map as Oscar looked on. The rest of their team already had been briefed and were keeping an eye on their targets. They were the last to arrive, so were meeting there.

"Any questions?" Bruno addressed each man with a stare.

"Who's left guarding the brothels after the johns leave?" Jasper asked.

"Only two men, and from what we've been told, one goes to sleep soon after they lock the doors."

"We need to hit them just as they throw the last guy out." This time Roman got into the conversation. "If we wait, we'll have to storm the door, which will give them more time to react and call in reinforcements."

"What if I went to the door pretending to be a last-minute customer?" Jasper suggested.

Roman tapped the desk with his index finger. "I like that idea but your face is pretty well known around here. Oscar, you do it. See if you can find a different shirt to wear in the car."

"Will do, sir."

"I'll have the maid bring you one of mine. If they see you in all black it might tip them off." Bruno sent a message on his phone to his staff.

"I can do it," Arlo interjected. Why, he didn't know. Maybe he wanted to prove something to Layla's father, or maybe he just wanted to feel useful. The waiting around had him on edge.

"No, Oscar will. You have someone waiting for you. Osc is single," Roman interrupted.

Bruno's head popped up from his phone. "You have a woman now, Arlo?"

Again, Roman spoke up, "Layla and he are quite close."

"Yeah, but that is all for show." Her father frowned.

"I would say it is more than show. Wouldn't you, Arlo?" Jasper grinned and slapped him on the back. "By the looks of the kiss she gave you before we left, you two are pretty hot and heavy."

Bruno's eyes narrowed. "Actually, I think it would be best if Arlo did go to the door. He has more experience."

At that moment, the maid came in holding a red t-shirt in her hand. "You two decide, I'll wait in the car." Arlo took the shirt and left.

His shoes were silent on the dark wooden floors as he walked to the front door. Rinaldi basically just said he was expendable and someone that he wouldn't mind getting shot. What was that man's beef with him, anyway?

"Hey, wait up," Jasper called from behind and he stopped just short of the front door. "I'm ready to get out of here also. Time to blow shit up."

At least Jasper always made him smile despite the situation. "Yeah, this is dragging on way too long."

"I just heard from Dom. He's heading back now." He ended up staying until one, and knowing Dominic's dislike for crowds and being around people, it was probably the longest day of the poor guy's life. "The girls are not supposed to call but put it on vibrate just in case."

He knew all that anyway but Arlo knew Jasper was just there to keep him company.

"You're a good friend, Jasper."

"I know." He flashed the bright smile that made the girls notice. "What's Bruno's beef with you?" He ran a hand through his dark hair.

"Hell, if I know." Arlo exhaled. "I better put this on."

"No, you're not." Roman's voice echoed down the hallway. "I want Oscar to go to the door. He's least known around here. I'm not taking any chances."

A red-faced Rinaldi trailed behind. "Let's get into place. I'm going with you."

They decided at the last minute to just hit the one brothel, the one where Tonya had been held. They had the most intel on that place and there was too much of a risk for the ladies at the others getting killed in the crossfire. Tonya had given them a detailed layout of that location as well.

Oscar dropped the guys off about a block away before parking in front of the building. It was in a low rent area. A few places were decorated with boarded up windows and sketchy characters hanging around on the front steps. The humid night brought out the lingering smell of urine and garbage to the fullest. It was a good bet that Fedor also ran drugs in the neighborhood. They would have to be fast and not raise any suspicion that would cause someone to call in reinforcements.

They were all wired for sound with earphones in place.

Arlo witnessed Oscar park their vehicle and get out. Jasper and Bruno were by the back of the building in case anyone tried to make a break for it. Roman was up front but on the opposite side of the door from Arlo.

Oscar staggered up the few steps of the house and rang the doorbell. "Anyone home?" He began banging on the wooden door.

A man from inside threw it open. "We're closed."

"I need to get flayed," Oscar slurred.

"Are you deaf or drunk? I said we're closed." The guy grabbed Oscar by the shirt and began to shove. His eyes widened when Oscar pushed him back in the house and held a knife to his neck. Roman and Arlo rushed in and shut and locked the door behind them while Oscar slammed the guy against the wall.

"Name," Roman demanded.

"Joseph." The man's gaze darted about the room.

"Are you carrying?"

When the man didn't answer Roman, Oscar poked the blade in far enough that it drew blood.

Slowly he nodded. "My back waistband."

Oscar pulled the guy forward and Arlo reach for the weapon to unload it. "How many guards are here?"

Joseph glanced up to the ceiling and sighed. "Just Yuri. He's with a girl. First room on the left, second floor."

Grabbing the guy by the arm, they led him to the kitchen, where they gagged and bound him to a chair. Roman let Jasper and Bruno in on what was going on.

"Let's go." Roman motioned to Arlo as they quietly climbed the stairs. The place was quiet except for the squeak of bed springs bouncing in the room Joseph had named. They stopped, one on each side of the door. "On three," Roman whispered and then held up said number of fingers to count down. When he got to one, Arlo put his foot to the door and crashed it in. Yuri lay on the bed with a woman on top. He reached for the gun on the bedside table but Roman fired first. They had a silencer and the bullet hit the man square in the forehead. They couldn't risk the woman being held as a hostage.

"Nice shot," Arlo congratulated him as he reached for the woman and put his hand over her mouth. "Shh, it's okay. We're not here to hurt you, we're here to rescue you."

The woman trembled, her eyes wide from shock, fear, or both.

"Do you know Tonya Yerkhov?" She nodded.

"She sent us to rescue you. If you promise to not scream, I'll let you go." The woman swallowed and slowly moved her head again. Arlo cautiously let her go. Seeing a robe nearby, he tossed it her way and she covered herself.

"Who are you?" Her dark hair shaded her face as she tightened the belt around her waist. The fact that she hadn't even glanced at the dead man in the bed spoke volumes.

"I'm Roman Caponelli, and you are?"

"Kara." Taking a seat in the only chair in the room, she crossed her legs and reached for a cigarette. Her fingers shook as she put it to her lips and stuck a match.

"We're at war with Fedor. Once we get the guards out of here, call the police. Tell them that the men had been stealing money from their boss and ran off. Let them know that you've been held here against your will, forced to work as prostitutes, and that there are other houses like this out there."

After blowing a ring of smoke, Kara snuffed the cigarette in the ash tray and stood up. The old floor creaked as she strolled the few steps to the bed. Kara spit on the body of the dead man as a tear started to roll down her cheek.

"You're free now." Arlo placed a hand on her shoulder and her tough exterior crumbled.

Her lower lip trembled. "Thank you." Her shoulder jerked as she sobbed. "Thank you so much."

# Chapter Twenty

It was four in the morning before they finally left the brothel. Everything had gone smoothly. The money was collected from the gambling sites, and the warehouses had been emptied. A few of Fedor's men had died in the exchange of gunfire but none of Roman's had been hurt. They'd contacted Dominic again with updates just in case any of the ladies had awakened and wondered where they were.

Joseph had lunged at Oscar in the kitchen when they untied him, and he'd received a bullet to the gut. Kara found them blankets to wrap the bodies in and they loaded them out the back door of the building and into their vehicles. Roman gave her the number of a lawyer to contact in case she or any of the girls had any trouble or needed help. As soon as they shut the back door, they could hear her happily calling for the other girls to come downstairs and that they'd be going home soon.

After a stop at their Chicago crematory to dispose of the bodies and to drop Bruno off at his house, they were on the way home. It was a job well done and they were all on a high and eager to get to Genoa. Arlo couldn't wait to see Layla but would she be happy to see him? It was an asshole thing he'd done when they left. His only excuse for his behavior was that he was on edge and if he didn't return, it was his hope that if Layla really did have feelings for him, that might kill it and she'd move on without him more easily.

None of the guys had called their women but he noticed each, with the exception of Oscar, had contacted Dominic to ask about them. They were about thirty miles outside of town when he finally gave in to the impulse to text their man at the house and see what was going on.

*Arlo: Dom what's new?*

*Dominic: What's new? Serious fucker? Can't a guy get some sleep?*

Shaking his head, Arlo knew the guy was tired but weren't they all? Next time, they could send Dom, and he would stay home with several beautiful women, a big screen TV, and all the beer and food he could eat.

*Arlo: You got more sleep than we did, dumbass.*

*Dominic: Get to the point. Like all the other pussy-whipped guys, I expect you're calling about your woman.*

*Arlo: Not whipped and not my woman, but*

*yeah, I want to know about Layla. Did she sleep well? Is she with Madison?*

*Dominic: Don't know. She left soon after you did.*

What the hell? Screw this! Arlo dialed Dom's number and a few seconds later Dom answered.

"Are you kidding me? Christopher said you are almost here and yet you call? I can't wait to go fucking home but I don't want to wake Stephanie," he grumbled.

"What the fuck do you mean Layla isn't there?" Arlo grit his teeth. He was in the backseat now and both Roman, in the front, and Jasper beside him, turned to stare.

"Yeah, I did everything you said. Sat at the bar forever. Which I am never doing again. I think they wanted to call the police on me for loitering but were afraid to deal with shit if they did." The guy didn't like to talk much so for him, this was a mouthful.

"Where is she?" Arlo made a fist.

"I didn't find out until I got back here that she was gone. Madison said she was upset and wanted to leave."

"Where is she?" The woman was a hard head, that's for sure.

"Madison finally relented but only after she insisted Layla take one of the guards with her."

"Where'd they go?" Chicago? A hotel? Arlo laid his head back on the headrest. He'd gone too far and messed up. They'd probably passed her on the

176

way back to Bruno's. Son of a bitch, he'd lost her before he even had her, and it was his own damn fault. There was no way he could drive himself back to the Windy City. He could barely keep his eyes open.

"She's at your place," the voice on the other end finally answered.

"What?" Did he hear him right? He could barely see straight he was so tired.

"I guess she said she wanted to go home so Tony drove her there and agreed to stay until you got back."

Relief hit him like a sledgehammer, but then… "Who. The. Fuck. Is. Tony?" The grip he had on the phone tightened. He was close to throwing it out the window if he didn't find out in 2.0 seconds.

"When none of the guards here would go with her, she called in one of her dad's. He came all the way from Illinois to get her."

Arlo closed his eyes and pinched the bridge on his nose. Layla was pissed and wanted the hell out of there, that's for sure. "Thanks, Dom. I'll touch base with you soon." Ending the call, he tucked the cell in his pocket, and tapped Oscar on the shoulder. "I need you to drop me off at my place first."

"What? I want to see Jackie," Jasper whined. "Then we can all go back there together."

"Layla's not there, she left the compound last night with a guard."

Roman cursed. "What? I left strict instructions for them all to stay there. Who the fuck took her?"

"Some Rinaldi man named Tony." He cursed and shook his head.

"Drop Arlo off first," Roman relented. "It's on the way."

The lights of Genoa came into view and they all let out a collective sigh. Home sweet home. It wouldn't bother him a bit if they never set foot in Chicago again but that was just another one of the issues he had to work out with Princess Rinaldi, and His Royal Highness, Bruno.

Sunlight started to peek over the horizon. He'd been up for almost twenty-four hours. Oscar had been pounding energy drinks, so the guy would probably be too wired to sleep even when he was able. Only a few cars roamed the streets as they turned down the drive to the Caponelli estate. They made a brief stop for Arlo to get out. Few words were exchanged as they were all exhausted and ready for bed.

He waved as they left the parking lot and he took a brief look in the black SUV with Illinois plates. There was nothing of interest inside and no trace that Layla had ever been in there but she obviously had. What'd possessed the woman to leave the security of the compound?

Dragging himself inside, he took the elevator to their floor, being way too tired for the stairs. As soon as he opened his door, the cool metal of a gun barrel touched his cheek.

"Who are you?" the gun owner inquired as he pushed the gun in deeper and it rattled against Arlo's teeth.

"I think the question is," Arlo smiled as he shoved his gun into the guy's stomach, "who the hell are you?"

"Tony Rinaldi." The young man lifted his chin.

"Arlo Brunetti. You're in my home." Not to mention two seconds away from losing his shit.

The guy lifted the gun in his hand and raised the other in a mock surrender. "I'm glad you're here so I can finally leave." Stepping back, he holstered the gun under his jacket.

Arlo held open the door. "Then get the hell out." The kid was only doing his job and as long as Layla was safe, he shouldn't be angry but the thought of another man being there alone with her all night didn't sit well. Tony grabbed his phone from the kitchen counter, nodded in Arlo's direction, and walked out the door.

The lights were on but she was nowhere in sight. That meant she had to be in the bedroom. That was a good sign, right? She couldn't be that upset if she was sleeping in his bed. Peeking into the room, his heart broke and melted itself all at the same time. Layla lay there in one of his shirts, mascara had streamed down her cheeks from crying. Taking deep breaths, he flexed his fingers and briefly closed his eyes. Not wanting to wake her, he quietly turned the light off and lay on the couch. Their relationship was as complicated as the one with the Russians.

For the first time in a long time, it felt like they'd gotten a handle on that situation. Now if only his relationship with the woman in the other room was that easy. Resting his head back, Arlo immediately fell asleep.

\*\*\*

## *Layla*

Soft snores coming from the other room awoke her. Tony? If her cousin was asleep, her father would kill him. The man was supposed to stay there and protect her until Arlo returned. Bolting upright, she tossed the pillow aside. Was he here?

Tiptoeing to the doorway, her heart jumped for joy. He was home and looked to be unharmed. Her feet sank into the plush rug as she rounded the couch where he slept. Arlo appeared relaxed and younger than she'd seen him in a long time. Leaning forward, she pushed the hair back that had fallen in her face. They had much to discuss and way too many secrets.

She gasped when he snatched her hands and held her in place.

Arlo's eyes widened as he slowly let her go. "I'm sorry. I was half asleep and you startled me."

Layla dropped to her knees and rested her arms on his knees. It was up to him to make the first move. His lack of response to her when he'd left had caused her to doubt everything she'd started to believe. That they had a future and that she meant something to him after all.

Reaching down, Arlo lifted her into his lap. His strong arms wrapped around her, pulling her close. Tension eased out of him as she melted into him. Layla rested her head against his before finally raising it to look into his eyes. His callused finger traced along her jaw before moving his palm behind her neck to pull her close. Arlo's lips touched hers in a fierce kiss. One of longing and lust. Instantly she enveloped him with her arms, pressing her chest against his. They kissed for a long time but it would never be enough.

Coming up for air, she broke the embrace and rested her arm across the back of the couch. "So, you do care?"

"Never said I didn't. It's you I wonder about." His gaze landed everywhere but on her.

"Hey." She placed her hand on his face to get him to look at her. "I swear to you on my life I never meant what you overheard. I was just messing around with Maddy. I care about you more than I have any man. I've wanted to be with you for so long. I think we have a future together but what the hell was that when you left? Do you realize what a wreck I was?"

"Fuck." Arlo frowned. "I'm sorry. I never meant to make you worry."

"How could I not? We were scared to death for all of you but you just walked off." She waved her hands and shook her head. "What the hell was that?"

Arlo sank into the cushions. "Who the hell is Tony?"

"Stop trying to change the subject." She rose from his lap and fisted her hands at her hips.

"No, you tell me who he is. I know he works for your father but have you been, you know, together?"

"Oh, for crying out loud." Layla paced, if she wasn't barefoot there would have been a good chance she'd kick something. "He's my cousin, and since when do you care after the way you said

181

goodbye last night?"

Arlo got up and stepped in front of her. "It's because I do care that I didn't want to say goodbye." He growled and walked over to the window. "All my life, when people I loved hugged me before they left..." He turned around and his voice cracked as he spoke. "They never came back."

# Chapter Twenty-One

### *Arlo*

"What do you mean they never came back?" Layla went to his side.

Arlo placed his hand on the cool glass of the window. Outside all was peaceful as people strolled by below on the walking path or cruised around in boats. If they had any chance at all, they needed to be honest. They had many obstacles to their relationship, so he needed to get past this one.

"I was a wild kid. A typical boy, I guess. My mom had her hands full with me."

"And this has what to do with what we were just talking about?" Layla was losing patience with him. Hell, she'd waited for him all night and here he was stalling. Never had she looked more beautiful standing there wearing nothing but one of his dress shirts.

"I'm getting to that." He took her hands in his again. "I was a kid but old enough to stay alone. My mother got a phone call. A friend of hers was sick and needed to go to the hospital. Neither of my parents were big into affection, but before she left, Mom stopped and hugged me to her chest. It took me by surprise. I didn't even know what to say. I was in shock. Both my mom and dad had grown up in mob families, they were tough and all business, so this was out of the ordinary for us both. Mom looked at me one more time before she left and said, 'be a good boy.' She ruffled my hair and left." Taking a deep breath, he stared at the ceiling. "On the way to her friend's house, she skidded on an icy spot in the road and hit a semi head on."

Layla gasped and put her hand over her mouth. "I'm so sorry. I thought it had been a car accident but I never heard the specifics. That still doesn't explain your behavior toward me."

"After that it was just my dad. As you know he worked closely with Mr. Caponelli, so I spent a lot of time at Roman's."

"Like father, like son," she added.

"Something like that. One night he was acting very agitated, not like his usual self. He had a job that night. It must have been an important one as he never acted that way. Right before he walked out the door, he did the same thing my mother had. He reached for me and gave me a big hug." It sent a chill down his spine just thinking about it. Like someone had just walked over his grave. A premonition of bad things to come. "I waited up all night but he never came home. Around noon, some police officers came to the door. I found out later that they'd found his body in the river. Head bashed by a bat or some such shit." He rubbed his forehead and returned to gazing out the window.

"What happened to you after that?" Layla enveloped him in an embrace from behind.

"I was alone and underaged. Social services were called but I left before they could return."

"Did you stay with family?"

"The only family we had were the Caponellis. I ran as fast as I could to Roman's house. Joseph knew, of course, and turned a blind eye to me staying in Roman's room most of the time. He pretended I wasn't really living there and often invited me to eat at the table with them."

"Is that why you two are so close?"

"That and several other reasons." He'd give his life for the guy.

"Years later—I was seventeen at the time—I overheard Joseph on the phone in his office. They had found out who killed my father. I had a name and an address. That night Roman and I snuck out. We'd run with his father's men enough to know what to do. Roman took a couple of weapons from the gun safe and we left at midnight hoping to settle the score."

He could still feel the fear that raced through his veins. Neither had killed before but it had to be done. There was no proof so they could go to the police but if they made the man confess, justice would be served.

"What happened next?" The heat from her body meshed with his. She was his equal in every sense but the one that was most important to her father.

"We were two tough kids who were scared shitless inside. After driving twenty minutes to a

185

suburb, we found the place that he lived. It wasn't a rival mob family but the home of a used car salesman's house. We could be in and out without causing a stir, he was the only one there. Come to find out, my father had been sleeping with the man's wife. He found out who he was, followed him after he left a bar, and hit him in the head as he walked along the river. It had nothing to do with a job. The man had contacted him and wanted to talk."

"I'm so sorry you had to go through that."

"You and me both. Anyway, when push came to shove, I couldn't kill him. Roman shot him in the head and we left out the back door. We were young, stupid, and had no clue what we were doing."

"What happened next?"

"We were nervous as fuck but feeling like we were kings of the street. Roman wanted a drink but we were underage. Old enough to kill but not old enough to drink." He chuckled and shook his head at their stupidity. "We robbed a fucking liquor store. Stole some cash from the register to make it look good, when it was a bottle of Jack that we really wanted." He tapped his index finger on the pane. *Tap. Tap. Tap.* "The next morning the authorities showed up at the Caponellis'. A camera had caught us both leaving the business. I confessed to the crime and did the time."

"Roman let you?"

"He wasn't there when they showed up. I owed him for what he'd done for me. Everything he'd done for me. Besides, Roman was going to college once we graduated. Had his whole life planned out.

I had nothing."

"So, you spent years in prison for a crime you hadn't committed?"

"I was an accomplice to a worse crime, just not brave enough to pull the trigger." Some of the weight he'd carried for years seemed to lift.

"It's quite the story. I'm glad you shared it with me but it still doesn't explain why you treated me the way you did last night."

"I guess I just have a strange way of dealing with things."

"I lost my mother too. She died of cancer and I hugged her every day." Layla said it to his back. "You didn't hug me because you were afraid you wouldn't be coming back? Like a superstition kind of thing."

Arlo turned around and framed her face with his hands. "No, I didn't hug you because I didn't want you to spend the rest of your life knowing that someone who loved you never came back for you." The hurt had gone both ways. He'd suffered for years not wanting to get close to anyone again. Roman was his only friend and he knew they would both kill and die for each other. They'd proved that many times over.

As Roman's wife, Madison was now included in that circle.

"Did you just say you loved me?" Layla pressed closer.

Damn, he hadn't meant to say it but he really did mean it. "Yeah, I guess I did."

"We've only been a couple for three days." She giggled.

"Sometimes you just know things are meant to be. I can't help loving you but I never dreamed you would feel the same way."

"I..."

Arlo pressed a finger to her lips. "Shh. Don't say anything now."

"But I want to tell you how I feel about you."

"Tell me when I least expect it. Like I said, I have issues. Issues that were made worse by what I overheard you say to Madison."

"I said it wasn't true." She stomped her foot.

"And I believe you now. It took a while but I do. If you say you love me now, it'll be because you're saying what you think I want to hear."

Layla groaned and shook her head.

"I'm not saying that I won't believe you, I just want to hear it when I least expect it."

"Whatever." Layla planted a big kiss on his lips. "You make me happy. Happier than I've been in a long time." She strolled away, her hips swaying in the oversized shirt.

"Where are you going?"

"To get dressed. I have a club to get ready to open." She stopped at the doorway of the bedroom. "Since I can't tell you how I feel, would you be open to me showing you?"

"Showing me?" Damn, she was beautiful and such a tease. Warmth flowed through his veins just thinking about all her soft curves.

Layla dropped the shirt to the floor. "Come to the bedroom and find out."

Arlo rushed across the room and Layla wrapped her arms around him as soon as he stepped through

188

the door. Her bare breasts pressed up against his chest. This was heaven for sure. Maybe he did die last night and just didn't know it. When her lips touched his, he knew he was still on earth. It was too good to be a dream. She tasted of cinnamon and some other spice he couldn't begin to comprehend. It didn't matter. His woman was here, that's all he cared about.

He grabbed her full ass and squeezed. Was it too much to hope for that she loved him too? The last thing he wanted was gratitude or an automatic response. When she said it for the first time, he wanted there to be no doubt in his mind.

Layla pulled back and pressed a finger to his chest. "About this no hugging when we say goodbye thing."

"Yes." He knew she wasn't going to let this go.

"We need something else. Something that is just our own to show we care but no one else will know."

"Okay, and what would that be?" He grinned at her concern over the problem they had to work through.

A frown crossed her face as she tried to come up with a solution. How she could think of anything while standing there naked had him baffled. The only thoughts in his mind were getting her into bed and under him. "I got it." Her eyes widened and a grin lit up her face. "We link pinkies."

"Pinkies?" He shook his head and laughed. This woman never failed to surprise him. Reaching out, he wrapped his pinky finger around hers. "There. Even if I have to leave you, this will always mean

189

that I'm coming back. No matter what. If I have to crawl my way back on my hands and knees from hell, I will."

She drew his palm closer and placed it over her heart. "You better or I will hunt you down and bring you back myself."

"Deal." Sliding his palm down, he cupped her breast. "Can we have sex now?"

"Arlo, I thought you'd never ask." The woman was a tease.

"I think you forgot that it was you who wanted to show me something." His thumb flicked her nipple.

Layla moaned. "What can I say? When you're around, I can't remember a thing."

"Then let me give you something that you'll never forget." Picking her up in his arms, he tossed her gently on the bed. She stretched like a cat and he nearly lost his mind. How did he get so lucky to have her here?

Never had he removed his clothes so fast in his life. As soon as he got into bed, she was on top of him. What a bear cat this woman was! He was the one that was supposed to be making love to her, but he wasn't about to say no to it being the other way around.

"And another thing," she started as she reached down to cover his hard length with her hand. "Don't pull the jealousy crap on me. You're the only man I want." Layla rose and drew him into her body. "And don't you ever forget it."

"No matter what happens, baby." He could barely speak as she began to move on top of him. "That's something I will always remember."

# Chapter Twenty-Two

## *Layla*

Draping her sweater over her shoulders, Layla took in the reddish colors of the sumac along the road.

"Do you want me to turn down the air conditioning?" Arlo already had his fingers on the dial. He always put her first and it sent a shiver of goosebumps down her arm. Someday, somehow, she knew it in her bones he would have to choose between Roman and herself and that was something she never wanted to happen. It was inevitable and she should have seen it coming. Arlo had mentioned it many times. Her father's issue with him was a mystery. He'd had no problem with her marrying Roman and his being a Caponelli but for some reason he hated Arlo. Whoever she married would have to help her run the family businesses and territories. All she cared about was being with the man she loved.

"You aren't coming down with something are

you?" His concern touched her.

"No, but it just feels like fall is coming early this year."

"You know how it is. Wait a day and the weather will change again." Even the sumac leaves had started to turn, as they usually did in late August. Little did she realize how quickly her time in Genoa would fly by.

"Yeah, that's true. I'm just not ready for colder temperatures." She bounced in her seat toward him. "Hey, we should go somewhere. Take a trip or something."

"You know we can't right now. The Russians have been quiet for a long time but that could change any minute."

Crossing her legs, she pouted. After the attack on their businesses, Fedor had been in and out of jail. There'd been no new attacks, however, any minute that could change.

"What are your plans for the day?"

"I have some things to do at the club." There was always something to do at the club.

"Layla, are you sure you want to run the place?"

"Yeah, why do you say that?"

"You could have opened it a month ago. It just feels like your heart isn't in it. Personally, I couldn't be happier. I don't like to think of you working there every night until late. We'd never see each other."

That was true. She enjoyed their evenings together and after the opening that would come to an end very quickly.

"What would you really like to do in life? What

is your dream? It can't be running a strip joint."

"It's not a strip club but you're right. I've run my father's clubs for so long, it's all I feel like I know how to do."

"You're a smart woman. I know you can do anything you set your mind to." Layla had to admit she'd never felt so comfortable with another person before. There was no doubt in her mind that Arlo would support her in whatever she decided to do in life as long as it was with him. "How long do you want to stay?" They pulled into the parking lot of the rehab center.

"How long will you be with Alexander?" Checking her phone, she noticed a missed text from Madison.

"Probably not more than half an hour." Arlo turned off the car, got out, and came around to open her door. Reading the text, she tossed the phone in her purse.

"Everything all right?"

"Just a text from Maddy. I guess there's a package at their house for me."

"A package?" His eyebrows arched. "From who?"

"Have no clue." She looped her elbow through his. "Guess we'll find out later."

Arlo escorted her to Tonya's room.

"Hi, Tonya." Arlo waved a hand in greeting and she waved back. Tonya had slowly warmed up to him but she was still nervous around men.

"I'll be back in forty minutes or less."

"See you soon." Layla kissed his lips. The guy had been a bit shy about PDA but she'd worn him down. Watching him retreat down the hallway, Layla felt like part of her went with him. They'd become two parts of one heart.

"When's the wedding?" Tonya tucked her leg under her knee.

"What wedding?" Layla smiled as she made her way to the easy chair next to Tonya's bed.

The young woman laughed. "You two, of course."

Layla brushed it aside, they hadn't talked about that yet. "Maybe someday. We have a few things to figure out yet." Digging into her bag, she handed the note from inside to Tonya. "For you."

It was barely out of her purse before Tonya plucked it from her fingers and squealed. Layla had been couriering letters back and forth between Christopher and his girl for weeks.

Tonya held the note to her chest. "How soon can we see each other?"

"I haven't heard anything yet." Roman wanted no changes in procedure until they knew Fedor was fully contained. "Hopefully soon."

"I'm just going to get a coffee and be right back." It was their usual routine. Give the girl time to read the letter in privacy, while Layla got something to drink. Entering the room again, Tonya was all smiles.

"Anything good in the letter?" Layla took her seat again.

"It's always good to know he still cares about me after all this time. I can't wait to thank Roman for all he's done for us." Any other mob boss would have killed Christopher on the spot for what he did to protect his woman. Roman was smart enough to use that love to work for them.

"Well, it's not over yet." Layla crossed one leg over the other. "Have you thought about what you want to do once you get out? Roman has a lot of businesses in town."

"No." Tonya hesitated and bit her lip.

"Well, if you don't want to work for Roman, I'm opening my club soon."

"What kind of club is it?"

"Arlo calls it a strip joint but it's actually more of a gentlemen's club, but we will have special nights for the ladies with male dancers." Her voice proclaimed her excitement but it didn't go all the way to her heart.

"I studied dance for years but I don't think that's the kind of dancer you're looking for."

"Really?" Layla exclaimed. "I took dance classes for years, too. Ballet, tap, jazz. Unfortunately, I had more desire than talent. Plus, I'm way too tall to be a dancer."

"I'd just gotten hired to a dance company back home. The trip here was to celebrate that success, but now because of my injuries, I'll probably never be able to dance professionally again."

It was true. Her legs had both been broken and she still walked with a slight limp.

"You could teach." As soon as she suggested it an idea lit up like a light bulb in her head. Her brain buzzed with ideas. That was it. Instead of a dance club, what about a dance school? "Really, can you teach?"

Tonya glanced toward the ceiling before turning

her attention to Layla again. "I'm sure I could. I'd have to see what qualifications I'd need to be certified but like I said, I've taken classes since I was a child. Why?"

"I just had the idea about starting a dance school. I don't have the skill to be a professional, but I still love it and want to be involved somehow. I could be home at night as well."

"But you know kids have class during the days, so you would have to schedule lessons in the evening as least a couple nights a week."

"Anything would be better than getting home after midnight."

"I like that idea." She rose and walked to the window. "Let me look something up online and see what I would need to be qualified. Is there a school in town?"

Layla stood up also and went to her side. "No, but there should be and we should run it."

Tonya turned her way, her smile the brightest she'd seen since coming there. "Yes, we should."

\*\*\*

*Arlo*

Rubbing his chin, Arlo sat in the vehicle and stared at the safe house. They couldn't keep Alexander here forever. They either had to kill him or use him to get back at his brother. The change in the man had been nothing short of a miracle. He still couldn't comprehend that they were the same person. When he'd first laid eyes on Alexander

196

when he'd kidnapped Jackie, the guy was a psychopath monster. He didn't even look the same, especially in the eyes.

Under the careful supervision of the doctor, the Russian had become a new person but was it real? Could he be trusted? Carrie swore it was but had he conned her also?

Easing out of the SUV, Arlo glanced around the neighborhood. They'd gotten a handle on the surveillance situation but it would be too hard to believe that Fedor didn't have any idea where Alex was. They hadn't acted on it, so who the hell knew.

Knocking on the door, Arlo was soon let in. As usual, they'd known he was coming. It had become a weekly ritual. He'd dropped Layla off to visit Tonya while he spoke with Alex and his keepers. The man was no longer behind glass but had a monitor strapped to his ankle. The doctor had him earning privileges like he was at summer camp or some such shit. It seemed messed up but who was he to say otherwise.

"Guys." Arlo pulled out a chair and took a seat at the table. "Would you mind if I chatted with Alex in private?"

"Sure, we'll be in the kitchen." The two guards left.

They were about the same size. In a fight it would be a pretty even match. Alex hadn't flinched when he'd used torture on him. Today, he wasn't so sure that would be the same result.

Alex was the first to speak. "What are you going to do with me?"

"Not sure yet." Arlo picked up the deck of cards

that lay nearby and started to shuffle it.

"Any word from my brother?" He cracked his knuckles.

"Nope. The law is keeping him busy."

"Good, but you'll hear from Fedor again. He needs me back or he'll lose control."

"You think so?" Arlo set the deck in the middle of the table.

"Let me at him and I will take him out of the picture."

"I thought you couldn't kill him."

"I'll think of something. The bastard fucking poisoned me. Look would he did to me. Turned me into a crazy person."

"Well, from what the doctor said, you were already crazy. He just helped it along." Arlo wasn't letting him off easy. The Bratva men were legends at cruelty.

"That's true. She's a saint and I'm a sinner. Still he needs to be put down like the dog he is."

"What do you think we should do with you?" Was he playing good all along just to get free?

"Let me go," he insisted.

"Not going to happen." Arlo snorted and shook his head.

"You can't keep me here forever." No, they couldn't. It was costing a fortune in security, not to mention the rent and other expenses involved in keeping him here.

"We can do anything we want. Would you rather be dead?"

"No, let me out and I will make sure there is peace between the Italians and the Bratva."

"You can't make promises you can't keep." This was a waste of his time.

"I would keep that one," the guy insisted while looking him straight in the eye.

Arlo groaned and leaned back in his chair. "I need more info. Something I can take back to Roman. Something that shows we can trust you."

Alex rested his elbows on the table. "My brother is very vain. He thinks all women love him."

"What good is that information?" Frustrated, Arlo cursed and threw the deck on the floor.

"I'm sure it will come in handy someday." Alex bent to pick up the cards. It was one of the few pleasures the guy enjoyed there. When all the cards were accounted for, he placed them back in the center of the table. "Give me a piece of paper and pen."

Spying a notebook nearby, Arlo pushed it across the table. The man wrote some numbers down and shoved it back. "What's this?"

"A secret account Fedor has. Tap into it and you'll have him right where you want him. He loves money more than anything."

"We take his money, then what?" Arlo folded the paper and put it in his pocket.

"He'll strike back." Alexander seemed sure of himself. "But you'll be ready for him."

"What's in this for you? If we get Fedor and his money, your organization will be in ruins."

"It already is but I can bring it back. With your help, of course."

"Again, why would we help you? You must be crazy."

"Fedor made me crazy but he really is. I would like nothing better than to take my rightful spot as the head of the family again. I am the oldest and deserve to rule. You make that happen and I will be loyal forever. We'll never trouble you again. You have my word on it."

Taking a deep breath, Arlo studied the man again. He didn't trust him, didn't like him, but they couldn't kill him in case they needed him. It was a bad game they were playing and he had no idea who was going to win. In the back of his mind, there was a nagging feeling they would need Alex someday and he hadn't the slightest clue which way the man would go when that happened.

# Chapter Twenty-Three

## *Layla*

"How was your visit with Tonya?" They were now on their way to Roman's.

"Good. She's anxious to leave and get on with her life." What that poor girl must have gone through these past months. "I hope once she and Christopher are reunited, they can move on with things and be a normal couple again."

"Me too," Arlo echoed her sentiment.

"Who knew you were such a romantic?" Wiggling her eyebrows, she smiled at her man. Yes, he was her man whether he was ready to admit it himself or not. He had a kind heart despite the hard exterior. Tonya's idea for a dance studio still buzzed in her mind. It would be perfect but she wasn't ready to give up her club just yet. What kind of qualifications would she need to open a school? Maybe visiting her business one more time might put things in perspective. The club would take more of her time away from Arlo than she wanted. For once in her life, her thoughts were more about how it would affect someone else instead of herself or the family business. Whether it was from maturity or love, did the reason really make a difference?

"I just want peace. I'm getting too old for this shit," he grumbled.

"You're not old but I agree with you." Living day to day, always looking over your shoulder for threats was wearing them all down. Even Roman clearly wanted the issues with the Russians settled before his child was born. Things were quiet now but any second Fedor could strike back and end someone's life.

They waved at the soldiers guarding Roman's gate.

"What did you want to do again?" At first, she thought he was only concerned with her whereabouts but it finally dawned on her that Arlo really cared about what occupied her mind and time.

"Remember, I wanted to go to the club?"

"That's right. What's left to do? I thought you'd be open by now."

Arlo'd been distracted ever since his visit with Alex but then so was she. What was there left to do? She had all the employees hired. Marketing was done. Supplies all ordered, and yet she'd dragged her feet. Not willing yet to give the go.

"I don't know. My heart's just not in it."

"Really?" His eyes perked up. He'd made it perfectly clear that he didn't want her to do it but the decision would ultimately be hers.

"We'll see." There were a lot of things to

consider. What about her father and running his businesses, she couldn't do that from here. The club was an impulse purchase. Granted it would make money, but would it make her happy?

Dominic and Jasper waited by the front door.

"Hi, guys. Where are your ladies at?" Stephanie and Jackie had fast become friends. They'd even started getting together once a week to do lunch and catch up with each other. That was something she'd lacked growing up in Chicago. It was hard having friends when you didn't get out much.

Jasper spoke for them both. "Jackie's at work and Stephanie is home working on another book."

"Really? That's exciting. Well, I mean the writing part. Not sure how exciting Jackie's job is but she seems to enjoy it," she rattled on.

"I'm pretty sure she's spending just as much time online planning our wedding."

"Oh, and when is that?" Seeing as Jasper had proposed on the boat after Dominic and Stephanie's reception, she'd not heard a lot about when that would happen and had truthfully been a little afraid to ask.

"We're not in any rush." The guy brushed it off but the shy grin told otherwise. "Who knows? Maybe we'll just up and elope to Vegas someday."

"You should have a wedding here. It's tradition." Arlo's answer could have knocked Layla over with a stick. Since when did he care about wedding traditions?

"Just because Roman, Valentina, and Dom all had weddings here doesn't mean it's a tradition we all have to follow." Jasper raised his chin.

"We're family, and a family celebrates major events together," Arlo reinforced his point.

"And family accepts when some members want to do things differently." Jasper shook his head and headed into the building with Arlo right on his heels.

"That's bullshit. If you're getting married, have the wedding here so everyone can attend."

Layla gawked as she witnessed something she'd never expected to see. Two tough made men arguing over wedding details. Her gaze locked on Dominic, the only man still standing outside with her.

Dom remained silent but just motioned with his hand for her to go in first. He obviously thought the sun rose and set on Stephanie but the cleaner for the mob didn't bother wasting too many words on others.

Pushing her sunglasses up on her forehead, she looked around for her sister.

"Maddy's not feeling well." Roman poked his head out of the office. "Would you mind checking on her upstairs?"

"Of course." Her foot was on the second step before he addressed her again.

"And Bruno sent you a package. It's on the table in the dining room."

"Oh, thanks. I'll grab it before I leave. Probably just some paperwork to sign or my mail." Hurrying up the stairs, the click of the office door closing echoed as she reached the top.

Maddy had suffered with morning sickness the first few months of her pregnancy and the second trimester hadn't been any easier. Knocking lightly, a weak voice from inside welcomed her in.

The curtains had been drawn and the TV played quietly in the background. Madison hit pause on the remote and told Layla to have a seat.

"How are you feeling?" The greenish tint to her skin and the bucket near the bed spoke volumes.

Madison's growing belly rose and fell with her deep sigh. "The same. Mornings are hell and seem to last until around five in the afternoon, then I start to feel okay. Is it five yet?" She at least still had a sense of humor.

"Have you seen a doctor?"

"If I would let him, Roman would have one here twenty-four-seven." She settled into the pillows and reached for a glass of water. "Every pregnancy is different. The doc said everything is fine. I just need to take it easy, rest, and hope it goes away soon. Like I said, usually around five in the afternoon, I start to feel better."

"Five! I couldn't handle that." Layla wore a path in the carpet. Everything had started to weigh on her mind. Her concern for her sister, the ongoing battle with the Russians, the club, and where her relationship with Arlo was headed.

"What's going on with you?" Madison pushed down with her palms so she could sit up a little higher.

"Here, let me help you." She rushed to her sister's side.

"I'm fine. Just tired of lying down."

"Here, let me comb your hair." Spying a brush nearby, Layla sat on the bed and began to brush

Maddy's long hair. How she missed having the chance to do this as kids. The missed opportunities of getting each other ready for prom, first dates, and other major events in young girls' lives made her heart ache. It just reinforced her resolve that she needed to make some major changes in her life.

"That feels nice. I must look a mess but Roman, bless his heart, tells me every day that I've never looked more beautiful." She bit back a sob. "My hormones have me crazy. I cry over anything. Those Hallmark commercials are a bitch to get through."

"I've never been pregnant but I'm pretty sure that is normal as well. I'm afraid I can't get through one of them myself without bawling."

Maddy took Layla's hands in hers. "I can't tell you how happy I am to have you here. Please tell me you'll stay permanently. I know Arlo and you are getting close. Do you think he's the one? I so want it to be true."

"I want it to be true also but it's complicated. We have some serious concerns to work through."

"I have full confidence that no matter what it is, you two will end up together," her sister insisted. "I know it in my heart."

Layla sat back in her chair and crossed one knee over the other. "First, I have to figure out a few things in my life. What is most important to me and what things are keeping me back from reaching that goal." And what to do with the damn club she'd invested so much of her father's money in.

"So, what's stopping you?"

"Well, nothing, I guess." It was true. She could

sell it. The place looked great and was ready to go.

"Then don't waste any time sitting here with me. Get your life in order and go get your man." Madison was adamant.

"Yes." Nodding her head, a thrill went through Layla's spine. "I need to stop waiting for things to fall into place and do it myself." This was important to her. Maddy was important to her. Arlo was important to her. Every day, Lake Genoa felt more and more like home. It was easy to picture herself living and raising a family here.

"Then what are you doing here? Make it happen." Madison insisted.

"Yes. I will." Layla tightened her jaw and stiffened her spine.

"Good. Now go get your shit together so you can be here to help me figure out all this baby and kid raising stuff. I can't imagine not having you involved in our son's life."

Layla's head popped up. A boy? "You're having a son? Roman's got to be pleased beyond belief." Visions of toy trucks and blue blankets popped into her mind.

"Yes, I have a feeling he'll be handing out a few cigars at the meeting today."

"I'm so happy for you both." Layla couldn't resist hugging the soon-to-be mom. "You need to feel better soon so we can get some shopping done. Now that you know the sex, we can decorate, pick out clothes. Squee! I can't wait to hold my new nephew."

"I can't either but first things first. You need to make arrangements to move here. Permanently. I know Dad wants you to rule the family but it's going to be twice as hard for you as a woman. Their ways are the old ways and they will test you more severely than they would a man. Even Roman said that."

"I know." Her gaze fell to the floor. "I know."

"And I know he doesn't want Arlo to leave. They're like brothers and we are sisters." Her eyes started to water again. "Call me selfish but I want you here."

"I want that also." But telling her father was going to be a nightmare.

"Then what are you waiting for?" Maddy slapped her hand on the bed and Layla jumped. "Go out and make it happen."

"Today?" She couldn't help but laugh at her sister's enthusiasm.

"Not just today. Now."

"Ah, okay." Layla slowly rose to her feet.

"I mean it. Do whatever you need to do to make Arlo yours and keep your ass here. I need you. I really do." Maddy reached for the tissue box.

"You know you can count on me for anything."

"I know, but I also know some things take time and Father isn't going to be easy. He'll have to get used to the idea that his daughter isn't going to be a don and he'll need time to find someone to take your place."

"I will give him a call next week. I promise."

"Not next week. Now." The expectant mother's eyes were wide and staring her down.

"I know. You're right. Don't put off until next week what can be done this week," she humored.

Her nerves were getting the best of her. Never did she want to disappoint her father but spending her life doing something she had no interest in would be like living in prison. What if she regretted it? Once she told him her thoughts and that she wanted no part of the family business, as far as being its leader, that is, what would their relationship be then? Could he forgive her and accept Arlo as her husband? Decisions, decisions. Her head hurt just thinking about it.

"Yes, I'm older, so I'm right." The woman in the bed finally smiled. "You can do this." She reached for her hand.

"I can." Layla placed her hand on top of the one holding hers.

"And you're going to start today."

Layla rolled her eyes. "And I'm going to start today."

"You know I'm only doing this for you. Well, and my own selfish reasons."

"You're right, Maddy. I'd never be happy going back to Chicago. It would be the end of Arlo and me. I could never ask him to give up his family for me and half of my family is already here. Father will just have to get used to the idea. Right after I do." She knew in her heart it was true but there was one thing she had to do first.

"Change is never easy but it's usually for the best." Her sister took a drink of water. Already her color was starting to return to her face.

"I have to get going, Maddy. Will you be all right by yourself?"

"Of course." She nodded toward the phone on

her bedside table. "All I have to do is call and Roman will have anything and everything I need here in a matter of seconds."

"You're a very lucky woman." To think that years ago Layla was supposed to marry Roman. Thank god that never came to fruition. They would have been terrible together while her sister and he were a perfect match.

"I know, and you are too. Arlo loves you so." Maddy had spent more time with the man in the last few years than she had. They were close. Like brother and sister, similar to the way Layla felt about Roman. It was as it should be and was meant to be.

"Have you told him yet how you feel?"

"I've not said the three little words but I do know something I can do that shows how much I care."

"And what's that?" Crossing her arms in front of her chest, Maddy wiggled her eyebrows.

"Not that. Well, at least not yet today." Shaking her head, she smiled at her sister. "I have something else in mind." Taking a step back, the smile on her face grew. She knew exactly what she needed to do to make him happy, but first she had to make sure it was what she really wanted. "I have to go. We'll talk later. Love you."

"Love you, too."

Shuffling down the stairs, her feet barely touched the steps. Bypassing the office, she went straight for the door and ran right into Oscar.

"Oops, sorry, Miss." Oscar had manners but it sometimes made her feel ancient.

"That's all right." She paused with her hand on

210

the door handle. "Aren't you supposed to be in the meeting?"

"I was but I needed to check something on one of the cars."

"Are they expecting you to return?"

"No."

"Can you drive me somewhere?" Arlo would be livid if she left on her own.

"Of course. Where to?"

"I have to go somewhere." The handle of her purse had fallen off her shoulder and she put it back in place. "I just need someone to drive me. We can take my car."

"I can do that. Sure." He halted before adding, "Did you get the package that was here for you?"

"Oh no. Thanks for reminding me. It's something from my father."

"I know right where it is. Meet me in the car and I'll be right there." Somehow the stress of the last few months seemed to lift from her shoulders. Staying here and giving up the leadership of her father's crime family was the right thing to do. Taking a final stroll through the club she no longer wanted to own was a step in the right direction also. Layla had just been going through the motions. Doing what she thought would be a good business venture, and it would have been. It just wouldn't be best for her and Arlo.

Oscar opened the backseat door and placed the priority box on the seat. The vehicle shifted when he settled into the driver's seat and started the engine. "I'm afraid I don't know where you want to go to."

"Just drive and I'll let you know."

"Do we need to alert Arlo to where we're going?"

"No, I want it to be a surprise." She felt almost drunk with happiness about the future.

"I'm sure he will be." Oscar put it in gear and drove out of the yard.

"It never hurts to keep a man on his toes." Layla wiggled hers, feeling like a kid out for a joy ride.

It was only a short drive to the club but with each mile they drove, a sense of unease grew. It was a mistake not letting him know where she was. All their phones had trackers but Arlo had had hers removed, stating that he couldn't risk others knowing where she was. He was with her at all times anyway so maybe that was why something didn't feel right.

# Chapter Twenty-Four

"Ma'am, I don't feel comfortable about this." Oscar had a death grip on the wheel. The man was intense there was no doubt about it. Being the new guy on the job made that a given and she'd basically made him go against orders. His boss would be mad as hell but he'd just have to deal with it. There was no way she could handle being stuck in the house any longer. Like Maddy said, it was time for action.

It was a beautiful day and being inside any longer would have caused her to go bat shit stir crazy. More importantly, it was time to take the bull by the horns and take control of her life once and for all. Everyone had been on alert for months and nothing had happened, so why would it make a difference if she took a quick trip to her club? Let's make that former club. There, she'd said it. Layla didn't want it anymore. Still they weren't supposed to be taking any extra chances and that was what was probably really bothering the man next to her.

"It'll be fine." Her head throbbed and the bright sun didn't help it either. "I'll take full responsibility, when and if anything happens, which I seriously doubt it will."

He flexed his fingers on the steering wheel. "Whatever you say, ma'am."

That irked her even more, maybe it had been a bad idea not to wait for Arlo. At least she'd taken someone with her. She was being careful. Smart. "Please don't call me ma'am. It makes me feel old."

"Sorry ma—ah, Miss." Now he was even more flustered. Great, that was her fault for sure. With her luck, they'd probably have an accident. Something odd like a turkey flying out of nowhere and crashing into their windshield. At least it was still summer and they didn't have to be watchful for deer. "It's just that we're still at war. I should have left word."

Layla sent a quick text to her realtor to meet her there. She was taking a chance the woman wouldn't be busy but for what she would make on a possible new sale would get her notice. Vicki responded within ten seconds.

"Don't say that." Her fist clenched and a knot formed in the back of her neck. The men in her family didn't always let her know everything that was going on. Yes, there was always trouble brewing somewhere but they'd been able to keep ahead of it. Until they blew everything up at the wedding.

"It's true." Oscar wasn't giving up.

"That's debatable. Nothing's happened since we went after Fedor." Thankfully. "It's just a pissing contest between a bunch of men trying to see who has the bigger dicks. It's stupid, really. He's up to his eyeballs in trouble with the law. The guy's probably fueling his private jet to leave the country right now." If only that were true.

He grumbled but remained silent. Oscar was young. Probably just out of college if he'd gone at all. She didn't really know him that well and that had made it easy to get him to do her bidding. Everyone else would have put their foot down about her being an easy target and staying out of sight. It was just her luck to run into him in the hallway.

Her gaze fell to her hands. A manicure was way overdue but when had she had the time lately? Maybe that's what she would do later. She glanced out the window again and smiled at a field full of sunflowers. It'd been such a happy summer season so far. Weddings, new mothers-to-be, and engagements. It was time for her to experience all those happy moments as well. Now, if only she could just convince the man she wanted to undergo them with her.

The men in the family were hardly ever home lately. Too busy keeping an eye on their territories and interests both here and in Chicago. Chewing on her fingernail, it dawned on her that maybe things hadn't been as calm as they'd led her to believe.

"Where did you want to go anyway?" He slowed as they neared an intersection.

They'd made a brief stop at the Java Shop for coffee and a pastry to go. "My club. Or should I say soon-to-be former club." She punched the address into the GPS on the dash.

"I heard something about that." He constantly monitored the side and rear-view mirror, a common trait of those that were always on the lookout for danger. "What do you mean by former?"

"I decided I wanted to do something else." Like have a life.

"Better to decide that now before you get any more invested into it."

"That's what I thought. It will be an easy sale, I hope. Everything's basically all set up. I even have the menu set, bar licenses, employees hired."

"Hmm. Maybe Roman should buy it." Oscar seemed to ponder it over. "Heck, maybe I should."

"Really? You'd be interested?"

"I'd have to talk it over with Roman. He's looking for more legit businesses to invest in."

"You should, and if you ever need any help, I'd be just a phone call away. Think it over." The leaves on the trees along the road were just starting to turn. At least the sumac was and the maples would soon be next.

Oscar tapped his fingers on the wheel. "I'll mull it over but I still think it's a bad idea to leave the compound without letting someone—"

A vehicle came out of nowhere, blocking their way. Layla braced herself with a hand on the dashboard. The tires squealed as the vehicle skidded to a stop. They'd barely come to a halt before four men surrounded the SUV and tore their doors open. The barrel of a gun was held firmly to her skull. Her heart dropped to the pit of her stomach. So close to having everything she dreamed of only to have it end today.

"Careful. Ever so careful, unbuckle your belts." Layla didn't need to see his face to know it was

216

Fedor. The accent and deadly vibe said it all. Oscar's arm flexed next to hers. The last thing she wanted was for him to do something to save her.

"Do as they say." Her shaking fingers fumbled with the seat belt release. "Please."

Oscar let out a deep breath, or was it a groan? As soon as they were unbuckled, both were dragged from the truck and thrown on the hard blacktop. The flat surface of his boot was on her face. Tiny rocks and sand dug into her hair and skin. "Not so high and mighty now, huh, bitch?"

"It takes a big man to bully a woman." Layla talked tough but she'd never been so scared. After taking his foot off her face, Fedor pulled her to standing none too gently. Her bare leg was scraped and most likely bleeding. Acting on instinct, Layla hit the bottom of her palm to his chin. The jolt knocked him back a step but didn't lessen the hold he had on her.

"Shoot him in the leg." The Russian gangster ordered and the sound of gunfire deafened her ears as she screamed. She couldn't look. Couldn't bear to see one of Arlo's friends dead on the road. He groaned and her eyes flew open. Oscar rolled around on the hot surface clutching his leg with both hands. Blood seeped between his fingers.

"No." She didn't recognize the moan that escaped her lips but knew it was her own.

"Yes, you do as I say or your friend here dies." The hot air of his breath hovered by her ear. It took three men to hold Oscar down. "Understand?"

Vigorously she nodded her head, and said yes. "Please don't hurt him." This was all her fault, and if Oscar died because of her she'd never forgive herself.

"I never said that." Fedor motioned and they shot the other leg. Oscar's scream would haunt her for days to come. If she had days, that is. It was hard to move. Hard to breathe. Hard to think. She wanted to run to him but worried what would happen if she did. "Take his phone and toss the keys." His henchman did as he was told while her captor rushed her to their truck. One of her heels lodged in a crack on the road and it remained there. Pain shot through the sole of her foot as she stumbled and fell to the ground. "Grab your fucking shoe."

Looking up from where she'd fallen, her jaw tightened and her eyes narrowed. "They will kill you for this."

"They can try but they won't."

Two men, one on each side of her, lifted her to standing and ushered her to the extended cab of the truck. Layla turned to see where Oscar was. He remained on the ground, now on his side, his face a tortured portrait of pain. At least he was still moving. As if reading her thought, Fedor turned her around to face him. "I left him alive to tell Roman we have you."

"Why not just tell him yourself?" She bit her lip fighting to take the words back that had just left her mouth. The last thing she wanted was to anger him further.

"Because that's how we play the game. It's his turn to come to me."

"What makes you think he will want me back?"

"They will want you back. Your father, your

sister, your brother-in-law, and your fucking boyfriend, Arlo Brunetti. Now get in the damn truck." They shoved her in there and one threw her lost shoe at her chest.

\*\*\*

### *Arlo*

Inhaling the bootleg Cuban cigar, Arlo relished the deep rich favor. Not a smoker, he did enjoy the occasional fine cigar and they had good reason to celebrate. Roman shared that his first child would be a son. The Caponelli heir would be born soon and they all couldn't be prouder.

Just as quickly as the good news was shared, they were back to business. The struggle with the Russians just wouldn't go away. Fedor had been cleared of sex trafficking and running brothels. Ryan had passed on firsthand information he'd received from law enforcement friends in Chicago. How the hell did that happen?

"I don't get it," Jasper griped, a large cigar hanging from his lips. "I'm sure he has a lot of law in his pocket but this is clearly illegal and totally messed up."

"Apparently whoever is on his payroll created a paper trail that didn't lead to his door." Roman puffed out a circle of smoke. The guy was proud as could be about becoming a father and wasn't about to let anything dim his mood.

"I visited Alex today and he gave me the numbers to Fedor's accounts. Once we empty them, he won't be able to buy a newspaper," Arlo admitted.

"We need to kill him." Dominic stretched and placed his biker boot-clad feet on the coffee table.

Roman glanced at Dom's footrest and scowled. "Yes, and not soon enough."

"I say we strike Fedor's compound." Jasper voiced his opinion. "Take the fucker out, once and for all."

"I agree. This has been going on for far too long." Roman leaned forward and set his stogie on a crystal ashtray. "I'm talking to Bruno in," he glanced at the Rolex on his wrist, "a few minutes to discuss the specifics. Several other families will be involved as well."

"Good." Jasper nodded.

"What about Alexander?" Arlo had mixed feelings about the man. Granted he was the brother to their enemy, and a killer, but anyone in this lifestyle was. Not the brother part, but the killer part. Everyone in this room was, yet they had wives and girlfriends who thought differently about them. Loved them anyway.

Layla, as the head of her family, would be expected to deal out punishment, retribution, and death. She may be the daughter of a don but he knew Layla didn't have that in her and he, himself, had a conflict with Bruno even considering putting her in that heartless position.

"He will need to be put down." Roman interlocked his fingers and set them on the desk.

Arlo's chin hit his chest.

"I still think he could be useful. The man did

give us the locations of several prime businesses and we were able to free all the women from those horrible brothels. And what about the account numbers I just got?"

"That remains to be seen."

Arlo jumped when the cell phone buzzed on the desk in front of them. Speak of the devil, Rinaldi was on the line. Rubbing the back of his neck, he made eye contact with Jasper. Something felt off. He had nerves of steel, yet they were quivering under his skin. Something was wrong.

# Chapter Twenty-Five

The meeting lasted forever, at least it seemed that way. Arlo tugged at the neck of his shirt. Only seeing Layla would relieve the tension flowing through his veins. His phone rang as soon as he left the office. An unknown number.

"Hello."

"Mr. Brunetti?" It was a woman, the voice faintly familiar.

"Yes." He wandered to the living room in search of Layla.

"This is Vicki. I'm Layla's realtor. I met you a while ago at her club and she left your number as a contact."

"Right. Yes, yes, of course. What can I do for you?" The room was empty.

"Well, Layla asked me to meet her here and she never showed up."

"What?" He stopped. A pain in his chest throbbed. "Where is here?"

"The club. She called for me to meet her here but it's been half an hour. I tried her cell but there's been no answer."

Arlo raced from room to room but there was no Layla in sight.

"I'm afraid I have to leave for a showing and I can't stay any longer. I can't get ahold of Miss Rinaldi to let her know."

"Layla's here somewhere. I'm sure she forgot about the appointment. I will let her know."

"She just called me an hour ago and was very excited about meeting here."

"Really? An hour ago?" That was weird. He took the stairs two at a time. The woman was probably giddy about baby stuff with Madison and forgot about it but why would she be meeting the realtor today? She'd not mentioned it all despite the numerous times he'd asked what her plans were for the day.

"Yes, she said she had some exciting news for me so I'm a bit concerned that she's not here but I can't wait any longer." The coo of birds in the background proved she had left the building.

"I'm sorry for your inconvenience. I'll have Layla get back to you as soon as possible."

"Not a problem. I'll be in touch. Thanks so much, Mr. Brunetti." Arlo could hear the engine of her car start and the door slam.

"You're welcome." Arlo ended the call and knocked on the door of Madison's room. She called from inside for him to enter. His boss's wife sat in bed, a book in her lap and a glass of water in hand.

"Sorry to bother you but I'm trying to find your sister." He had no intentions toward Roman's wife whatsoever but stayed by the doorway out of respect.

"She's not downstairs?" Setting her glass on the table, she scooted back to the head board.

"I didn't check everywhere, I just figured she was with you."

"No, she was but left about a…" her gaze fell to the clock on her nightstand, "maybe a couple hours ago. I don't know. I must have dozed off for a bit."

"Probably in the kitchen getting something to eat." He hoped. "I'll check there." Reaching for the door he added, "Sorry to bother you."

"No bother." He started to close the door but Madison called out. "Arlo?"

"Yes?"

"I'm so happy you two are finally together." The smile on her face was genuine.

"I am too. Thanks, Maddy."

Rushing downstairs, he peeked in all the rooms. No Layla. Sprinting to the kitchen, he nearly collided with Jasper, a donut dangling from his mouth and a cup of coffee in each hand. "What the fuck, Ar?" He managed to get out before carefully taking the pastry in one cup-filled hand.

"Is Layla in there?" A feeling of doom overwhelmed him.

"No, just Dom."

"Ahhhh." He couldn't help the groan that escaped his mouth. This wasn't like him to be overwhelmed with fear. She was in the house somewhere, she had to be.

Turning around, Roman stood staring at him. "What's going on?" Roman came toward him.

Smoothing his hair back, Arlo exhaled. "Just a

224

bad feeling. Layla called and set up a meeting with a realtor an hour ago but never showed up. I can't find her anywhere in the house."

Roman called the gate house while Arlo paced. When he glanced back his way, Arlo knew. Layla wasn't there.

"Fuck."

The phone in his pocket buzzed and he nearly ripped it apart trying to get at it. "Yes."

"It's Vicki." Her voice high pitched and shaky. "We need help."

A chill went down his spine. "Who needs help? Layla? Where are you? What's going on?"

"No, she's not here."

He let out a breath and stuck his fist against the wall.

"But there's a man here. He's been shot."

"Who?" If he didn't start getting answers soon, he was going to fucking lose it.

"He refused to let me call 911 until I called you first."

His eyes locked on Roman's. A stern expression on his face as the man said something in Jasper's ear.

"He said his name is Oscar. He's been shot." Her voice cracked as she panted into the phone.

"You did the right thing." He tried to remain calm while wanting to jump out of his skin. Where. Was. Layla. "Let me talk to him. Please."

"I can't, he passed out. They shot him." Now she was crying. "There's blood, so much blood. I don't know what to do." Vicki sobbed.

"You're sure Layla isn't there? Did Oscar say

anything about her?"

"We tracked Oscar's phone. I have a location and men on their way." Roman put a hand on Arlo's shoulder, the support easing the stress and making him focus.

"No, he barely got his name out and said to call you before he passed out" she cried. "He's still breathing though, so that's good. Right? There's so much blood."

"Stay calm. Help is on the way."

"I'm afraid. I don't know what to d-do," she stuttered.

"I know, but we have men coming. How soon?" He voiced to Roman and he held up two fingers. "They'll be there in about two minutes. You need to stay calm."

Despite asking numerous questions, she knew nothing about Layla. He tried to keep her busy and asked her to look in the car. "Wait, I see her purse."

His knees went weak and he had to sit down.

"And a package in the backseat with her name on it."

He closed his eyes and prayed. Something he hadn't done in a long, long time.

"There's someone coming." She sighed. "Coming down the road."

"I'll stay on the line until they get there."

Roman's phone went off and he turned his back to answer it. Jasper had left and now returned with Dominic in tow. They stood to the side, ready to do whatever was needed. Vomit rose in his throat. If this is what love felt like, he wanted no part of it. He was near a break down and ready to tear apart this town brick by brick until he found Layla. There was no doubt now that someone had her. The same someone who'd shot Oscar. The same person who had tormented them for months. Fedor Fucking Dubnikov.

"They're here. I have to go." Vicki cut the line as Roman returned to the room. The expression on this face grim.

He didn't need to hear the name because he already knew in his heart it was true. Fedor had Layla.

***

### *Layla*

She awoke with a start. Visions of the past few hours rushed back. Poor Oscar, she whimpered. How could she live with herself if he died because of her impulsive actions? Reaching to rub her eyes, her arms wouldn't move. They were tied behind her back and her legs were tied to a chair.

"The princess awakes," Fedor spat as he paced the large room. It was a small warehouse of some kind. Rust dotted the floor in various spots, or was that dried blood?

Her stomach rolled when her gaze fell on a table of different weapons and what she could only assume were torture devices. The smell of sweat, fear, and bleach caused her to bend over as far as she could with her head between her knees.

Her captor grabbed a hunk of long hair and pulled her back up. Her skull needle-pricked with pain while she gasped for breath. The rapid movement just accelerated her nausea.

"If you don't want me to vomit all over your pretty shoes, you better let me go," she declared, sounding much braver than she really was. He abruptly let her go. "Why are you doing this?"

"The same reason I do everything." He strolled around her chair before stopping in front of her. "Power."

"That was the only reason you pursued me?" Right now she didn't give a damn but time spent talking was time he wouldn't be spending hurting her.

"Of course. The man that marries you rules a large territory."

At least Arlo didn't care about that, he wanted nothing to do with ruling. Some might consider it as lazy but it also meant not having to worry about putting your wife, daughter, or other family members in the same position she was in right now.

"What's your plan now? A quickie wedding?" Her stomach rolled again.

"The plan is to wait. I've contacted Roman and Bruno." He took a seat at the counter and picked up a knife. She swallowed as he used it to clean under his fingernails. "The ball's in their court now."

"How did you find me?" That was the thing that bothered her. They'd been so careful and Arlo had refused to have her tracked just for that very reason.

"The Caponellis should monitor their mail better. That priority box really wasn't from your father."

Dammit. How could she have been so stupid? She'd never even looked at it. "What did you ask for in return for me?" The last thing she wanted was to be used as a tool to gain wealth and territory from their years of hard work. All she wanted to do was go home but that wouldn't happen anytime soon.

"We'll see what they offer."

"And if they don't?"

"I believe they will." He walked in her direction again, and she tried not to flinch. "Especially after I start sending them your body parts."

Her mouth opened but no words came out. It was hard to catch her breath. There had to be something she could do, some way to save herself.

"Should we start with the fingers," he raised his knife, "or the toes?"

A cold sweat formed on her back.

"Maybe an ear?" He brushed aside her hair and the cold edge of his blade dragged along her scalp.

*Think. Think.* She begged for some solution to come to mind. He pulled on the shell-like part of her ear. Knife. Ear. Help. Knife. Ear. Wait a minute! There was someone else who had been very handy with a knife, Alexander.

"What if they have something better to offer?" His eyes shifted, looking everywhere but at her. His mannerism reminded her greatly of what Arlo had said about his brother when the man had first been captured. At least when she first met him, they did. Alex was practically normal now. If you could call anyone normal in this lifestyle.

"And what would that be?" He pulled harder and she could feel blood starting to run down the side of her head.

"Stop and I'll tell you." The pressure eased.

"Why should I listen to you?"

"Because I know something you don't." It seemed like forever but he finally let go and stepped back. "They have something you want and you don't even know it."

"I know everything that goes on." He laughed and tossed the bloody knife on the table. "Humor me with your last attempt to save yourself."

She lifted her chin and narrowed her eyes. "I don't need to save myself, someone else will and they'll kill you."

"Not likely." He grabbed the knife again. "You have two seconds to tell me why I shouldn't just kill you if someone is going to do the same to me." In two steps he had the knife to her throat. Her heartbeat pulsed through her veins.

"They have your brother," she panted. The only thing keeping her upright was the fact she was tied to the chair and he had a knife to her jugular.

Fedor eyed her warily before straightening. "I figured as much but thought they'd killed him by now."

"He's alive. Kept in a safe house." She gulped, in a rush to get the words out. "You can bargain to get him back. Alexander for me."

"And why would I want him back? I'm in charge now." Fedor seemed to weigh her words.

"Because if you don't, they'd tell everyone he's still alive. The oldest brother must rule from what I hear and that isn't you."

"But it should be me," he gritted out.

"I don't make the rules, your Bratva does." Her plan seemed to be working. "Roman's smart. He figured they might be able to use him someday."

"Son of a bitch." A groan echoed in the room as Fedor slammed the knife into the wooden table blade first.

"And that day is now."

# Chapter Twenty-Six

### *Arlo*

Things happened quickly but not fast enough. Fedor had called to negotiate with Roman and Bruno. Layla must have let him know his brother was in their hands. Hopefully voluntarily. It took years off his life just thinking of such a sweet woman in that monster's hands. If Fedor harmed a hair on her head, he would personally skin him alive, inch by inch, and then throw salt on his bare flesh.

Now they sat on the edge of a road, the exchange scheduled for midnight. The terms had been worked out. They each were only allowed one vehicle. Four men in each. Outside the one-mile limits, they had reinforcements. Arlo sat in front with Roman, while Dominic and Jasper took the back with Alexander between them. He'd been quiet the whole time, not even asking any questions.

They'd agreed not to tell Madison anything was up. Only that they'd found Layla and she was at home with Arlo. The woman didn't need the stress to cause any problems with her pregnancy.

Jasper patted him on the back. It wasn't too long ago that they were saving his woman from Alex, so he knew exactly what he was going through. The only thing probably keeping him from stabbing the guy next to him was that they needed the Russian alive to save Layla.

Christopher had drones monitoring the area. Roman received a text just moments before that Fedor was only a mile away. It was a battle between fear and happiness at seeing the woman he loved. Fear that something horrible had been done to her that he could never undo. Happiness that she was alive. No matter what, they would deal with it together.

"Show time," Jasper announced as headlights pointed their way. They waited inside as the oncoming SUV parked on the opposite side of the road about fifty yards away. When the doors of the other vehicle opened, they followed suit.

Roman and Arlo met Fedor and one of his henchmen at the halfway point. Fedor appeared relaxed and in control while he clenched his fists to prevent himself from tearing the bastard's head off. Until Layla was safe, he had to keep it under control.

"Where is she?" Roman asked. His boss only agreed to take him if he let Roman do all the talking. It was true. His head was about to burst and acting on emotion was never a good thing.

"Where's my brother?"

With that, Roman turned and motioned to Jasper.

He opened the door and Alexander got out. A tight smile crossed Fedor's lips.

"Layla?" Arlo couldn't remain quiet anymore. It brought a sneer from her captor and a glare from the man next to him.

Fedor nodded to the dipshit next to him and he returned to their truck. Opening the back door, he dragged Layla out. She appeared tired but unharmed. At least physically. She said his name and he whispered hers.

"How fucking charming," Fedor sneered. "Let's get this over with." He turned his back and walked back to his vehicle. When Arlo didn't move, Roman grabbed his arm. Not wanting to lose sight of her, he walked backwards.

Roman stood in front of Alex. "You are to meet halfway." Alexander started and Roman put a hand on his chest. "No funny business."

"Wouldn't dream of it." The guy smirked. "It's been a pleasure but I don't plan on seeing you again."

He started walking, as did Layla. She hesitated a few times, as if she expected someone to stop her. When no one did, her steps increased, her gaze never leaving his. Only a few more feet and she would cross paths with Alex and soon be in Arlo's arms. He took a step forward only to have Jasper hold him back. "You have to wait."

"I can't."

Jasper shoved him against the car. "Don't be stupid and blow things. You did the same thing for me not too long ago. Keep with the plan."

Nodding, he took a step back. Layla's scream

resonated in the dark night and his heart stopped. There in the spotlight of both their lights stood Alex, his arm with a choke hold on Layla's neck. Her feet barely touched the ground.

"What the hell is going on?" Roman shouted as they inched their way closer, guns now in their hands.

"Alex? What the hell?" Fedor approached with his men, armed to the teeth as well. "We had a deal. You for the girl."

"I'm making a new deal." Alexander swung around toward his brother, taking Layla with him, her feet wobbling in her heels.

"What's the meaning of this?" Roman yelled. "Fedor, we had a deal. A truce."

"Let her go," Fedor demanded of his brother.

"No. Now that I'm back, I make the rules," he declared through gritted teeth.

Arlo saw stars. Anger, rage, hopelessness. Every emotion you could think of battled it out in his brain. Only Jasper and Dom holding him back kept him from rushing over and prying her from his grasp. The Russian bastard had fooled them all. He hadn't been cured at all. He was going to be sick and the pain in his chest increased.

Fedor's bravado crumbled as he slumped against the side of their vehicle.

"We didn't kill you, Alex, remember that," Roman tried to reason with the man.

"That's correct, you didn't." He revolved around in their direction with Layla still held tightly to his chest. "But you did let your lacky there," he pointed at Arlo, "torture me several times. Maybe I should do that to someone he cares about."

Layla cried as her knees buckled.

"No." Arlo struggled to get out of his friends' hold. "Take me instead."

"I was hoping you would say that." Alex grinned as his eyes narrowed.

"Absolutely not," Roman argued.

"Alexander, no," his brother tried to reason. "I did all this for you. This is just going to cause a bigger war. Release the girl."

"You didn't know I was alive, so cut the bullshit. You've been waging war for months. Do you think I give a fuck about any of that?" Alexander turned around again and yelled. "Arlo Brunetti in exchange for Layla Rinaldi. If not, I break her pretty neck."

"No," Layla wailed again. "No, no. no." She struggled but he held her tight.

"I'll do it," Arlo yelled.

Roman pounded a fist on the hood and cursed. "Dammit."

Red filled his vision as Arlo imagined all the deadly things he wanted to do to this man. A man he'd started to believe had changed. What a joke it had been. Alexander must be laughing inside right now. The prick. The psychopath.

Roman approached him, his mouth a tight line. "I can't tell you what to do but I don't want to lose you. There's no guarantee we'll be able to get you back but I will promise vengeance."

"That's all I ask." He held out his hand to his best friend. "Take care of her."

"I promise. I know you'll find a way out of this. I'm not counting you out yet. Madison and I want you and Layla as godparents."

If it weren't so fucked up, he'd have laughed. Arlo grasped his outstretched hand and held it tight. "I'll figure something out. I'm not going down without a fight."

"I don't doubt that for a moment."

Jasper hugged him and whispered "Give 'em hell." Dominic just nodded and looked minutes away from having a melt down and killing everyone in sight.

After saying their goodbyes, Roman and he approached the pair in the middle while Fedor and one of his men met them there.

It happened fast. Layla was shoved into Roman's arms while Alex and Fedor grabbed Arlo. He didn't even get a chance to kiss her or have her in his embrace one more time. Just briefly his pinkie looped hers before they were pulled apart. Nothingness was all-consuming. The image of Layla fighting to get to him gutted him. Streaks of black mascara ran down her pale face. Her beautiful hair was disheveled and her clothing torn. Her cries raised the hair on his arms but other than that he was numb. Cold as ice.

It barely registered that someone had tied his wrists behind his back. He felt nothing. He had to be strong. In control. As the SUV's doors shut, it knocked the fight back into his veins. It had been a shock and betrayal that he was in this position but he wasn't through yet. The Russians had no idea who they just took.

\*\*\*

## *Layla*

Her life was over. They should've just killed her in the middle of the road because she couldn't go on living without Arlo. Oscar was still alive, or at least they said he was. Roman refused to take her to Maddy. His concern for his wife was admirable but she really needed family right now.

It was surprising they'd agreed to take her to Arlo's place, it didn't seem right waiting for him to return anywhere else. He would return to her, she knew it. He pinkie swore. It was childish and way too brief but it was all she had to hold onto at the moment.

Roman promised her they would monitor their location and make plans to get him back. The clock on the stove said it was two in the morning. After taking a hot bath, she curled up on the couch in a bathrobe, nursing a brandy, her phone in her hand.

A knock on the door caused it to nearly slip to the floor. She rushed to open the door, not pausing to see who it was first.

"Father."

"Layla." Bruno grabbed her in a bear hug. "I can't believe I almost lost you."

"It was my fault. I was so stupid," she sobbed.

Shutting the door, Bruno helped his daughter to the couch. "If it's anyone's fault, it's mine for not protecting you and keeping you safe."

"Don't start that now. You got your wish. Arlo's gone," she barked.

"That was never my intention." He frowned.

"You've always hated him and I don't even

238

know why."

It couldn't have shocked her more when he laughed. "It could have been anyone. It just happened to be him."

"What do you mean?" That he could joke at this moment pissed her off.

"You're my pride and joy and no man will ever be good enough for you. The minute I realized you were going to ask him to dance at your party, I knew he was the one. The one who would eventually take you away from me. It just took longer than I expected."

"I'll never leave you. You're my father."

"I know." He patted her knee.

"He traded his life for me." She rose and wandered toward the window. "I've lost the one I love."

"That's where you're wrong." He followed her there.

"I wish it was so."

"I know so. A man who gives his life for you. This man, Arlo. I know for a fact he will fight through the gates of hell to get back to you."

# Chapter Twenty-Seven

### *Arlo*

His face was on fire, but then that was a given since Alex had just hit him for the fifth time. His brother lounged in a chair by the wall. Fedor appeared relaxed but from the way he looked everywhere but at them said otherwise. Alexander was in his face again, screaming some nonsense in Russian that only the two of them could understand. Maybe that was a good thing. If he was going to be thrown into a vat of hot oil, that was the last thing he'd want a head's up on.

At least Layla was safe. Sweet, beautiful Layla. The only thing that bothered him besides not seeing her again was the fact that she would blame herself for his demise. His tormentor picked up a few tools off their torture table and the muscles in his stomach tightened.

"Imagine that, brother?" This time Alex spoke in English. "They tried to convince me that you were poisoning me. That paranoid schizophrenia ran in our family." Returning to Arlo, he bent over and got in his face. "Schizophrenia?" Rounding to his back, Arlo felt the cold steel of a knife placed in his hand as Alexander bent to whisper in his ear. "Do you think I'm crazy now?" Arlo kept his gaze to the floor but he could feel Fedor watching them. Alex spit and rose to go to his brother.

"What do you say to that, brother? Am I crazy?" Alex marched to his brother's side.

"It's bullshit. Mind games to turn you against me." Fedor still wouldn't look at either of them.

Hope surged as Arlo began to work the blade through the ropes that held him in place. Slowly and carefully. If he dropped it, they'd both be dead.

"That's what I thought. What kind of monster would turn me into a crazy person on purpose?" He chuckled and strolled over to the table.

Fedor flexed his fingers as he stared at the man's back. "I never trusted the Italians. Can't believe a word they say," he added.

"But I took your woman, Tonya. How can you forgive me for that?" Alex turned around, resting his behind on the table. "I'm so sorry about that. I wasn't thinking straight."

"She was easy to replace." He brushed it off. "I found another."

"Thing is, I don't even remember taking her or what I did to her. Just that I enjoyed it and couldn't wait to do it again. Imagine my misfortune to grab a Caponelli woman." He shook his head.

"As I said, easy to replace." Fedor swallowed. "Just like Layla would have been. We didn't need this guy."

241

"I'll kill you, you bastard." Arlo couldn't help himself. He was almost loose.

"I'm not talking to you." Alex warned before returning his attention to the man on the other side of the room. "I'm talking to him."

"Look," Fedor rose, "I'm sorry for what happened to you but I had nothing to do with any of this. You took off. I searched for you but you were already gone."

"How convenient for you." Alex narrowed his eyes and reached for a switchblade.

They started to circle each other. Careful steps, not too close and not too far away.

Fedor had to know he'd been found out. "Like I said, I searched for you. Hell, when I heard they had you, I took the Rinaldi bitch to trade for you."

Arlo felt the last strand of rope give way.

"Oh, and tell me, brother, how did you find that out?"

Rolling his shoulders, Fedor grit his teeth. "What does it matter how I fucking found out, you dumb ass? You're here, aren't you?"

"It matters to me. They had a doctor that treated me. After hacking into Father's medical records, I saw that he had it too. Unfortunately, he never told us and it runs in families. The illness is triggered by different things such as drugs and alcohol. Things easily put into my food and drink."

"So what?" Fedor got in his face. "We're both fucked in the head. What are you going to do about it, kill me?"

"I'd love nothing more." Alex grabbed him and turned his back toward Arlo.

"And you know we can't kill each other or everything is gone." Fedor fought to get loose.

"No amount of money is worth what you did to me. What you caused me to do to Tonya." Alex held him tight. "No one knows you're here except for the men that came with me. It'll be easy to kill them and no one would be the wiser."

"How about I kill Fedor, and Alex here lets me go?" Arlo held the knife to the man's throat.

"I like that idea best." Alexander smiled a very sane grin. The man had played them both and let Arlo win. A fist to the gut had Fedor bent over and out of breath. Arlo took the chance to tie the man's arms behind his back and toss him into the chair he'd just left.

"You can't do this," he pleaded with his brother.

"No, I can't kill you, but he can." Alex signaled Arlo's direction.

Surveying the selection, Arlo chose a drill but Alex placed a hand on the tool. "As much as I'd love to sit here and watch you put numerous holes in my beloved brother, we don't have time. It has to look like you escaped. Kill him quickly and hit me a few times in the face." He tossed Arlo some keys and a jacket that had been hanging on the wall.

"You're not going to get away with this." Fedor began to scream for help. It was useless, as the place was most likely soundproof.

"Shut up." Alex picked up a bat and swung it against the man's jaw. His eyes rolled back in his head while a few of his teeth littered the floor. "You have no idea how long I've wanted to do that."

"How do I know you're not setting me up

243

again?" The last thing Arlo wanted to do was walk into another trap.

"You could have killed me but you didn't. I owe you one." Alex reached out a hand. "Do it quick and get the hell out of here."

Arlo glanced from his hand to his face before reaching to shake it. It was odd but they'd been through a lot in the past couple of months and deep down, he felt he could be trusted. Fedor's moans broke the tension and returned them to the task at hand. "How will your people know you didn't do this?"

"I'll tell them the truth."

"The truth?"

"Yes, everything he did to me and everything you did for me but we don't have time to waste."

Shaking his head, Arlo marched over to his victim. The guy deserved to die. He was a brutal killer, poisoned his brother, which caused him to harm Tonya in unspeakable ways, trafficked women, and kidnapped Layla. Slapping the man's face to wake him up, Fedor slowly came back to life enough to plea.

"Stop, please," he mumbled before Arlo drew the knife and stabbed him in the neck. The gurgling sound of his life flowing from his body was the only noise in the room.

"Go. Now," Alex urged while telling him the directions out of the place. Donning the jacket and grabbing the keys, he rushed to the door before stopping and taking one last look at Alex.

"Thanks."

The man just nodded before pulling a chair next

to his dying brother.

Not waiting another moment, Arlo looked both ways and hurried down the hallway. Everything was right where Alex had said it would be. His knuckles were white on the steering wheel. He'd been given the gift of life in return for taking another's. It was a twisted life they led and it finally dawned on him why Roman was trying so hard to leave it. The man had a child on the way and the last thing anyone would want would be to see another fight for power like he'd just witnessed. It wasn't the same in their family but greed made people do terrible things.

He nearly drove off the road when his phone buzzed. Surprised he still had one, he fumbled around before answering it.

"Yeah."

"Are you free?" Relief surged through his body at Roman's voice.

"Did you know about this?" His friend always knew everything that was going on so it wouldn't surprise him if he did.

"I hoped but I wasn't sure he'd really go through with it," Roman admitted.

"Do you think next time you might give me a head's up?"

"What, and trust you to play the part? Last time I checked you hadn't taken any acting classes and I couldn't chance you giving anything away."

"Where's Layla?"

"Safe at home."

"Where are you?"

"A few miles out of Genoa. You can leave the car and ride with us. There's someone here who wants to speak with you."

"I thought you said Layla was home."

"She is. I knew you wouldn't want her waiting out here in the dark to hear if you were dead or alive."

He spotted Roman's vehicle up ahead in the shadows.

"Then who's there?"

"You'll find out."

"Dammit, Roman, I think I've had enough surprises for one night." He slowed to a stop.

Getting out, Arlo felt like he'd been through a battle and he had. The last thing he needed now was to see Bruno Rinaldi get out of the car. Groaning, he tossed Roman a dagger with his eyes.

"Don't worry, Arlo." Bruno walked to greet him. "I came to thank you for saving my daughter."

"You don't need to thank me for that. I'd do it again in a second."

"That's what I hoped you'd say. I haven't been that nice to you but seeing as Layla has her heart set on you, I thought we should get to know each other."

Arlo turned to Roman, who was biting back a snicker. "Now?"

"No time like the present. Get in the car, son." Bruno smiled.

\*\*\*

By the time they arrived back in Lake Genoa, Arlo was ready to pass out. He was exhausted, and relieved beyond belief. Fortunately, Bruno was kidding about spending the drive getting to know each other. They'd set a dinner date for Saturday night to celebrate their upcoming engagement. Layla didn't know it yet but after resting and spending all of tomorrow in bed, he was getting an engagement ring and proposing. He'd taken the time on the ride back to ask Bruno for his permission to ask for his daughter's hand in marriage and the man actually gave him their blessing.

As he let himself into the apartment, Arlo took in the scene of the woman he loved sleeping on the couch. She had one of his shirts on again and held a pillow tight to her chest. It was with fond memories he thought of how she'd chased him through the years. Well, she'd finally caught him and there was no place he'd rather be.

# Epilogue

### *Years later*

### *Arlo*

It was a serious case of déjà vu. Roman stood next to him at the bar in the Rinaldi mansion for a sweet sixteen party, only this time they both had grey in their beards and a few extra pounds around their waists. Bruno had passed away a few years ago from a heart condition so none of the original family still resided there. Connie had sold the place to one of Bruno's nephews and he'd offered the place up for the occasion. Mrs. Rinaldi now lived with Madison and Roman in Lake Genoa.

"I can't believe they still do this shit," his former boss groaned. Yes, he technically still worked for the Caponellis but Arlo was his own boss now. As of now about ninety-nine percent of the family business was legit. The winery was a huge success and the vineyard was known worldwide for the taste and quality of their grapes. They had restaurants in various locations from New York to California. Roman and Madison rarely left the Midwest but they made sure to keep a close eye on all aspects of their businesses with daily updates from all the managers at each locale.

The family sold the shipping business interests that they'd received from Stephanie's family years ago for billions. No one really needed to work anymore but that didn't stop them from being entrepreneurs. Arlo ran a security company with its biggest client being Caponelli Enterprises.

"It's tradition, and how could I refuse when it was at this same place and party that I first met my future wife." Arlo searched the room for the woman he'd loved for years. After confessing their love for each other so soon after getting reunited after the kidnapping they took it slow and married a year later. After much encouragement, Layla finally pursued her dream of owning a dance studio. She'd loved planning their recitals which he always attended and made sure to bring her a bouquet of roses after each one.

Layla fussed with their daughter, Angelina's, dress. It'd been a battle of wills for months between the two about what she would wear. Layla wanted something more age appropriate, while Angel wanted something red and more sophisticated. The two had finally settled for a dress somewhere in between. It was pink, simple, but also strapless. Arlo shook his head as he witnessed Layla tugging the top of her daughter's dress up to make sure everything was in place.

Arlo's eyes narrowed as he witnessed Roman's

oldest son, Joseph, approach the pair. Maddy had lost their first child late in the pregnancy and they'd adopted Joe soon after. Arlo had made it a rule that none of their kids could date before age sixteen so the kid had been counting the days until she came of age. At sixteen, Angel was just as beautiful and well-endowed as her mother on this special day. His daughter also had made it no secret that she liked the boy. Joseph was a few years older than the birthday girl but so had he been. At least Joseph excelled in school and had kept his nose clean. Fortunately, Roman and Madison were blessed with more kids and she insisted their children never join the mob.

"You know I'm going to have to kill your kid if he touches my daughter." Arlo shook his head and turned toward the bar.

"Yeah, you and what army?" Roman gave him a shove before pulling them both up a barstool.

"Just giving you a heads up on what's going to go down," Arlo joked and asked for two beers. After the bartender set them in front of him, he handed one to Roman and clicked the side of the bottle with his. "To family." Roman nodded and they both took a long swig.

He swiveled around again to face the ballroom. As his gaze roamed over the crowd, the corner of his mouth turned up. Everyone he cared about was there. The other two of their children were sitting at a table under the watchful eye of Madison and her mother. Angel had a younger brother and sister, Anthony and Erica. Angel was headstrong and wild whereas Erica was sweet and eager to please.

Anthony was a good kid and very interested in following in his father's footsteps as far as security went. He wouldn't be surprised at all if he ended up becoming a police officer. Anthony always kept a watchful eye on the women in his life and did what was right.

Madison leaned over to brush her hand across the forehead of their youngest. Roman and Maddy's kids sat nearby with Roman's parents overseeing their brood. They'd slowed down a lot but never missed spending any time with their grandchildren even though they lived in Florida for part of the year. After adopting Joseph, they went on to have two more boys and a girl. For being so terrified about trying again, Madison's other pregnancies had gone easy as could be. All their children were destined to be tall, dark-haired, and very successful.

At the next table sat Jasper and Jackie. As always, the guy had perfect hair and a flirty smile. Karma came back to bite Jasper. Forever the ladies' man, he was blessed with not one, but four daughters. Each one had him permanently wrapped around their little fingers. After the four girls, Jasper wanted to try one more time for a son. Jackie informed him she was done with having babies. He didn't seem to mind and currently balanced the youngest one on his knee feeding her cake. Jackie, after returning with a few more plates of dessert, placed them on the table and bent to kiss her husband's cheek. The expression on his friend's face glowed with affection as he gently squeezed her hand and drew her back for another.

Near the back of the room sat Dominic and

Stephanie. They still enjoyed living on the edges of society and being as close to being hermits as possible. Next to them sat Stephanie's father—yes, he was still alive and going strong. Dom had built a cabin nearby for the man and they visited every day. They also had children. Two miniatures of each. Their daughter was blonde and already a talented writer of children's books. Their son was also blessed with long fair hair and seemed to love blacksmithing as much as his dad. They hadn't had to use Dominic's services for quite some time but every once in a while, he'd get called up to make someone disappear either for the family or the MC club that they still joined forces with.

Even though they were seen as reputable business men of the community, it was the community that came first. None of them wanted to see their kids mixed up with bad influences so anyone that was found dealing drugs or doing illegal activity in Genoa would be dealt with to the fullest. The family still owned the garage out in the country and Dom still had a white van. It was newer but got the job done, the same as the old one.

Surprisingly, Christopher, the tech guy, was still alive and well. Even though he'd once betrayed them, he'd made up for it a dozen times over. In fact, he even worked for Arlo doing surveillance and monitoring the cameras. He married Tonya a week after they were reunited and they had two kids. Alexander insisted on paying for all her medical expenses. Since Roman had already taken care of that, he offered to cover all her bills to go back to school. That Tonya took. Christopher wasn't happy about it but his new wife said Alex owed her. After finishing up physical therapy she completed her education and was certified to teach. Tonya was the first person Layla hired when she opened her dance studio.

"Ladies and gentlemen." Layla's voice came over the loud speaker and Arlo's attention snapped back toward the center of the room. He couldn't have fought the smile that came across his lips if he tried. She was his life, his breath, his everything. Her fingernail tapped the microphone. "Can I have your attention?" She wore red, his favorite color on her. Her hair was still long and lush, her figure curvy and lean from years of dance. Arlo loved every minute he got to spend with the woman he loved.

"Thank you, everyone, for attending. We couldn't be happier to share this special moment with you. I know it is usually the father that does the speaking at these events but as everyone knows, my husband is a man of few words, and hates being in the limelight." There were more than a few chuckles from the crowd. Arlo felt heat rise to his cheeks. He crossed his arms in front of his chest and cracked a smile at his wife.

"The sweet sixteen party is very special for a girl and I know that I speak for my husband when I say we couldn't be prouder of what a bright and beautiful young woman our Angelina has become. It seems like just yesterday that I was here and asked Arlo to dance with me. Who knew that we would end up married many years later? A girl's first dance is a special time." She twisted to glance down at her daughter. "Angelina will pick someone to start the next dance and then you are welcome to all join in. Angel, who would you like to dance with?"

Arlo felt his stomach turn into a knot. How was he ever going to survive her getting married or moving away? He finally sympathized with Bruno and how the man felt about him all those years ago.

Angelina took the microphone from her mom and shaded her eyes with her hand as if searching the room for someone to waltz with. When her gaze landed on Joseph, a blush brightened her cheeks. "I choose Joseph Caponelli."

The crowd clapped and the young man stepped closer.

"Looks like our families will be joined together someday." Roman ordered another drink to rub it in.

"I'd like nothing better, just not today." Letting out a deep breath, Arlo took another drink. "They're too young."

"But before I do," Angelina started again, "I asked Joseph if it was okay if I dance with someone else first." The young man smiled and took a step back.

"What's this about?" Roman asked.

"I have no clue." Arlo sat up straight and tried to lock eyes with his wife but she was staring at their daughter.

"For years, I've watched someone special dance with my mother. He's made her so happy and I'm so proud to call him dad."

Arlo halted the drink next to his lips.

"He's always been there to wipe my tears, Band-

Aid bruises, and tell me to rise when I fall. I can't imagine any other man taking his place in my heart. I know someday, someone else will join his spot there but before that happens, I want my first dance to be with him. Arlo Brunetti, will you dance with me?"

It felt like he was having a heart attack but it was just his heart bursting with love. He turned briefly to wipe away the tears before standing and walking toward the dance floor. Layla still stood there and from the knowing grin on her face, she'd known this all the time.

When he reached them, he smiled at his daughter and drew his wife close for a kiss. Layla kissed his cheek once more before heading to the side of the room. Angelina gazed up at him, her eyes also glistening with tears. "I love you, Daddy."

"I love you too, sweetheart," he managed to choke out. The band started up and he managed to pull it together enough to waltz about the room. The third time around they stopped in front of Joseph. He was Joseph's godfather, and the more he thought about it, he could end up with a worse son-in-law.

"I think it's time for you two to dance." He shook Joe's hand and kissed his daughter's cheek. "I'm so proud of you," he whispered in her ear.

"Thanks, Dad."

Again, he choked up and only managed to nod at the two as they strolled to the center of the room. He stood for a moment and watched the young couple start to dance. Joseph played the perfect gentleman and Arlo had to admit, he loved that kid like a son also.

"Does this mean you're free to dance with me now?" He recognized her perfume before he heard her speak. Layla's arm reached around his waist from the back. Turning around, he embraced her in a tight hug.

"I'll be dancing with you forever." He kissed her sweet lips. God, he loved this woman. The occasion brought back so many memories. Why did life have to be so short? There weren't enough years to spend the time he wanted with those he loved but he was determined to enjoy and cherish every one for as long as they could. "Kids really do grow up too fast. I feel like the next time I dance with Angel it will be her wedding day."

"Hopefully that won't come too soon, but I know what you mean."

"Did you know about that?"

"Of course, but I had nothing to do with it. She came up with the idea." The slow dance ended and a faster one started.

"Care for a drink instead?" Taking Layla's hand in his, he led her from the dance floor.

There at the bar, the other guys had gathered along with their wives. Everyone was there. Roman and Madison, Dominic and Stephanie, Jasper and Jackie, even Christopher and Tonya were in attendance.

"Arlo, it's time for a toast." Roman held up a glass as the bartender poured glasses of Dom Perignon for everyone. The guy always ordered the best of everything. Layla reached for two glasses and handed him one. "To family. Whether it be by blood, honor, or marriage, we are all bound together

256

forever."

Shouts of, 'To family' and '*Alla Famiglia*' followed. Arlo found himself engulfed in hugs and kisses from the most important people in the world to him. He turned to see his other children still sitting and enjoying time with Connie and it made him think of his parents. He'd grown up with no one and now his life was filled with people who would never leave him.

This was family, his family. Those he'd kill for and those he'd die for.

"Are you all right, dear?" Layla laid her head on his shoulder. "You're so quiet."

He continued to soak in the love that surrounded him. "I've never been better, sweetheart. Never better."

**The End**

# About the Author

Ginger Ring is an award-winning author with a weakness for cheese, dark chocolate, and the Green Bay Packers. She loves reading, watching great movies, and has a quirky sense of humor. Publishing a book has been a lifelong dream of hers and she is excited to share her romantic stories with you. Her heroines are classy, sassy and in search of love and adventure. When Ginger isn't tracking down old gangster haunts or stopping at historical landmarks, you can find her on the backwaters of the Mississippi River fishing with her husband.

**Facebook Writer Page:**
Https://www.facebook.com/romancewritergingerring

**Twitter:**
https://twitter.com/GingerRings

**Webpage & Blog:**
http://gingerring.com/

**Amazon Author Page:**
http://amzn.to/1fslijd

**Pinterest:**
http://www.pinterest.com/Gingernovel/

**Instagram:**
https://www.instagram.com/ringginger/

# *Note From the Author...*

I love to write stories that take place in my home state of Wisconsin. The inspiration for the setting of this story is the beautiful tourist town of Lake Geneva. I changed the name to Genoa for the story but forgot that there is a real town called Genoa in Wisconsin. Both are beautiful places to see, so if you ever travel to Wisconsin, make sure to visit both.

There really is a Wollersheim Winery, and it's located in the beautiful community of Prairie Du Sac. I tried to do my best in remembering all the details I learned on my wine tour there, but you really need to see the place yourself. They also make some truly wonderful wine.

I hope you enjoyed this Caponelli family story, as there is more to come.

Join our Reader Group on Facebook and don't miss out on meeting our authors and entering epic giveaways!

# Limitless Reading

Where reading a book
is your first step to becoming
*limitless...*

LIMITLESS ♦ PUBLISHING *Reader Group*

Join today! *"Where reading a book is your first step to becoming limitless..."*

**https://www.facebook.com/groups/LimitlessReading/**

www.ingramcontent.com/pod-product-compliance
Lightning Source LLC
Chambersburg PA
CBHW030330200626
46816CB00006BA/1996